5/15

MW00954545

MOSQUITO CREEK INN

by

Sherrie Todd-Beshore

cover concept: s.t.p.

INDEX

CHAPTER ONE
Something Very Dusty

Dear Patrick, June 11…1997

       It all started when part of the wall gave way and Sonia fell, face first across the threshold of a hidden doorway…

       That night Sonia wasn't supposed to be trying on her mother's new shoes. After her mother left to show some houses and her grandpa went to Dr. Howes' for his weekly game of chess, she was supposed to put her younger sister and two younger brothers to bed, then she was supposed to finish a Girl Scout badge assignment, and then she was supposed to finish some ironing. But after the younger ones were in bed, checking out both pairs of her mom's fancy new shoes became Sonia's biggest priority.

       When she stood in front of the mirror with one green, high heel shoe on her right foot and one red, wedge heel sandal on her left Sonia was instantly taller. She fussed with her hair and twisted it into a knot high on her head. Suddenly taller and with her hair high up on her head she felt stylish, almost elegant… That is until she tried to walk.

       Watching her mother and her aunt walk in high heel shoes, it had looked easy enough. But looking at high heels and walking in them was like being on tippy toes held up by a nail. When she wobbled, she over corrected.

       Scrambling in a panic to regain her balance she grabbed for several of her mother's hanging dresses with one hand, and then stretched out for the back of the closet wall with the other. But the dresses came off the hangers and the wall opened up as if it was air.

3

After she hit the floor a whole lot of dust came up that made her sneeze. Her eyes watered and she blinked several times trying to see. Sonia wasn't hurt but the front of her bathrobe was a mess and she had to brush off the dust along with a lot of sticky cobwebs. That just made her sneeze again, and she still couldn't see very well.

There was only a single bulb in her mother's closet that cast more shadows than light. Squinting seemed to help her eyes adjust. In the dim light Sonia counted nine file boxes stacked on the far left of the small space she had discovered, with two very tall narrow boxes pushed to the right. There were two suit cases wedged side by side between the two tall boxes. The suitcases were the same size, but one was a dust covered blue and the other suitcase was grey.

At first she could hardly believe what she had discovered. Kids always think there must be a secret room, they even dream of a secret room but they rarely find one. This was where her mother hid the birthday gifts and Christmas presents, and the false wall was the reason Sonia had never found anything before.

All the boxes and suitcases were connected by major cobwebs and covered by a layer of dust, so she wasn't sure where to look first. But the suitcases were the easiest to reach without actually needing walk into the space behind her mother's closet, so Sonia decided to start with them.

On the blue suitcase she blew off the surface dust that covered just the top edge and the handle then wiped the rest with her bathrobe sleeve. The two clasps stuck a little but when she laid it down on its side she got the catches to release.

The lid flew open and a framed photo of her parents wedding was right on top. She didn't want to cry but tears stung her eyes when she lifted the picture. This photo disappeared after her father left when she was almost four. More family snapshots and mementos, just made her feel worse because their lives had gone on without him and she barely remembered her dad. Abruptly she reclosed the suitcase and pushed it back into place.

For a few seconds Sonia just stared at the grey suitcase, then on an impulse she pulled it out, wiped off the dust with her other sleeve and opened it too. On the very top was a large brown envelope with no address or any markings. But inside was the high school diploma of her mother's younger sister, Monica.

Below the diploma was a photo album with snapshots of her Aunt Monica as a baby, and then as a small child, and then a young teen. In nearly all of the photos, with Sonia's aunt, beginning at the age of four was a childhood playmate. The second name, hand printed on the back of each picture with the date, was...Zara.

Sonia got lost in the album and the snapshots and the funny comments written by her aunt of the shared experiences with her best friend as they grew up together. But without any explanation the pictures, train and theater tickets, bowling scores, post cards and report cards just stopped. After Aunt Monica's fourteenth birthday the rest of the album pages were empty.

She thought that was odd and searched for another album. But what she found was the front page of a newspaper that gave Sonia a real blunt explanation for the blank pages after her aunt's birthday.

THE MOSQUITO CREEK WEEKLY REVIEW   August 18, 1990
Mosquito Creek, Montana   Park Sullivan, Editor

...LOCAL GIRL GOES MISSING IN SEVERE STORM...

Sometime in the late evening of August 16, my fourteen year-old granddaughter Zara Grant, vanished.

Zara Grant was heiress to a vast, historic, family fortune. Her paternal grandfather Kohrs Grant reported her missing to local authorities. Mr. Grant became concerned when about an hour after Zara left her home at Grant Ranch to go riding, her horse returned to the ranch alone.

An immediate search for the teenager was hampered by a severe rainstorm that moved into the area with over 100 recorded lighting strikes throughout the night.

Sheriff, Jeff Howard, was interviewed by The Review. The sheriff stated that he did not suspect foul play as they expected to find Zara with the help of local tracking dogs. "That storm rolled in pretty fast." The Sheriff stated. "Her horse likely threw her and she is just hurt, maybe has a broken leg."

As the search for Zara progresses the Review will keep Powell County residents informed.

The face of the missing girl in the photograph published with the newspaper story, haunted Sonia. She hadn't known Zara Grant, but she felt sad that her Aunt Monica had lost a dear friend so young.

The sound of her grandpa's old truck coming up the driveway startled her back to the present - and her mother's closet - and it almost stopped her heart. Shaking, she fumbled to close the suitcase and close the small hidden door, and to re-hang her mother's three dresses and to fit the stupid shoes back in their boxes.

When Grandpa Molosky came upstairs to check in and say goodnight, Sonia was at the ironing board faking interest in some kind of game show blaring from the small television on her mother's tall dresser, while she pretended to iron.

She was so sure that her grandpa would hear the loud drumming of her heart that she was grateful for the noise of the television show and when he hugged her – she was even more relieved that he hadn't noticed the iron wasn't even hot.

CHAPTER TWO
Nothing Ever Happens Here!

June 12...

"Joker! No!" Eric Molosky's chubby arms tried to save his Aunt Monica's birthday cake from turning into his dog's afternoon snack. And Joker's large, flat paws left two damp-grass marks on the front of Eric's t-shirt, showing just how close he came.

When he spun around to avoid Joker - the four layer cake and the serving plate made a hard landing on the kitchen table. The top half of the cake slid sideways part way off the bottom half, cause Mrs. Molosky always spread her peach marmalade real thick between each layer.

"Yikes!" Eric over reached and almost did a shoulder plant in the cake but Joker jumped up again ready to play. He was knocked to the floor and his ear was immediately filled with Joker's wet tongue.

"You crazy dog!" Eric struggled to sit up. "Sit!" He got to his knees and peeked over the top of the table at the cake. It wasn't completely off the plate, but it didn't look good. "Mom's gonna turn us both inta stew!"

The Molosky's dog was a two-year-old mutt. Joker was part Cocker Spaniel, part Dalmatian and probably other parts too. He had curly, gold colored fur with uneven, black splotches. He actually looked as if someone had splattered paint on him.

When Grandpa Molosky saw the puppy for the first time, his shocked comment was, "That dog looks like a very bad joke." And the name, Joker, stuck.

After he got back on his feet, Eric led Joker to their glassed-in back porch then closed the kitchen door. Joker barked at Eric then ran out the pet-door to the backyard.

As serious panic set in both Eric's hands gripped the light brown curly hair on his head, while he tried to think. Somehow, he needed to slide the top half of the cake back across the bottom half, without breaking the whole thing it into a hundred chunks.

He figured that since the cake got lopsided, pushed too far one way, maybe he could fix it if he tipped it in the other direction. So he held the edge of the plate and the bottom half of cake in both hands and kept tilting it more, and more, and more until the top layers slid almost back into place.

Majorly relieved Eric set the plate down on the table and licked the icing off his fingers. His effort wasn't perfect. In fact the cake was still slightly off, but much better than on the floor with Joker's foot through the middle.

Mrs. Molosky's mini-van pulled up in front of the garage and stopped. The van doors slammed as he ran to open the back screen door. Ursula Molosky came through the door with a tangle of bags looped over each arm. She carried her purse by the handles clenched between her teeth.

For a small, slim lady she always seemed nervous. Her dark blonde hair generally looked like she'd just stood in a strong wind. Mrs. Molosky was generally rushed, and usually in a hurry. And that afternoon was no different.

But she wasn't in so much of a hurry that she passed right by the kitchen table. The lopsided layer cake and the icing mixed with some large crumbs, was impossible to miss. She dumped the grocery bags on the kitchen counter and then studied the cake, then looked at her son. "Had a little trouble spreading the icing I see?"

Eric shrugged. "I saved the cake from Joker."

"Joker!"

"He didn't lick anything."

Mrs. Molosky took some groceries out of the bags. "It looks dreadful." She emptied the first bag. Let's hope the decorations camouflage some of...of...this." Mrs. Molosky nodded toward the jinxed cake.

Eric rushed over to the grocery bags to be helpful and took two boxes of cereal to put away in their pantry. When he pushed a chair up to the top pantry shelf, he could see the cake from a higher vantage point. "How much decorations did you buy?"

Mrs. Molosky reached into one of the bags and removed candles, sprinkles and candy flowers. She lined them up on the table next to the pistachio cake that looked like a science experiment gone wrong. She studied the cake again, looked at her son, then back to the cake. "More icing," she decided. "It needs more icing. My younger sister will love that." She got another mixing bowl and then began to pull out ingredients to make more pastel green icing."

"Eric, I need you to put away the rest of the groceries but leave out the coffee so I can make up the big pot." Then she thought out loud. "Let me see, there will be seven of us for dinner and five more later, for cake and ice cream..."

"Mom, there's no coffee in any of the bags."

"What? Are you sure?"

"Yeah, I'm sure. Look for yourself." He shook all three bags upside down.

"It may have fallen out. Check the van, please."

Eric ran out the back door to search and then returned shaking his head. Mrs. Molosky made the face she always made when she struggled not to come unglued. When that happened she often talked to herself, mentally trying to reorganize everything. "How could I have forgotten the coffee? I can't leave again! I need to finish the cake, write up a listing on the Meeker house, then start dinner..."

She stood for several seconds with the faraway look that always worried her kids then she remembered Eric was still standing by the back door. "I know your brother Marc went with Grandpa. Where are your sisters?"

It took another second for Eric to realize she actually was talking to him. "They went over to the McKenna's house. Sonia talked Salina into going with her to help Gillian McKenna sew a skirt. But Sonia was *really* hoping that G-o-r-d-o-n might be home, too."

Mrs. Molosky blinked several times. More complications were piling up. "Sonia has a crush on Gordon McKenna?"

"She's in l-o-v-e!" He gestured out with both arms, with the kind of motive behind his smile that only a younger brother could have.

"She's only eleven! Gordon is only twelve! Good grief! Your sister thinks she's in love?"

Eric nodded pleased that his mother's attention was no longer focused on him and the state of his Aunt Monica's birthday cake.

Mrs. Molosky shook her head, then she checked her watch, then she checked the cake. "Ohhhh, I don't have time right now to deal with Sonia's budding romance. Okay. Get on your bike and ride to Anderlund's Market. Get a pound of coffee and see if you can find your grandpa."

Eric flew out the screen door, leaped down the steps in one jump and was down the driveway on his neon blue bike. At the end of the driveway he shot straight out onto the street, and skidded sideways to change direction toward the south end of town.

Anderlund's Market was part health-food and part art gallery. Carl Anderlund bought the town's abandoned train station and renovated it himself. According to local history the building had been there since 1909. It was a sturdy structure of pine logs and river rock.

Eric propped his bike against one of the posts that supported the wide front porch roof. The floor inside was also pine, thick, wide plank and original when the train station still shuffled passengers. Over the years the wood had warped slightly and it squeaked almost everywhere. The market always smelled of fresh dill and dried sweet basil.

Mr. Anderlund put the store checkout behind the former ticket counter, to the left of the double front doors. On the right just inside the front door was a giant metal birdcage that stood six feet high and three feet square. Inside the cage was Penny and Nickel, the two parakeets Mr. Anderlund won at the Butte Stock Show, two years before. He called them his "guard birds."

Every time a customer came in through the front doors the birds chattered and squawked and dropped stuff on the floor for several feet all around their cage. That day was no different and when Eric walked in seed husks crunched beneath his feet.

All the aisles and bins at the front of the store displayed county grown produce, organic canned and dried foods, along with locally baked breads, pies and cookies. At the back of the store were locally made candles, quilts, pottery, oil paintings and water colors, leather tooling, wood carving and weavings.

Eric spotted Leif Anderlund, standing on a short ladder organizing boxes of wheat-free crackers on a top shelf. "Where's your coffee?" Eric asked.

"My dad has all the coffee and tea on the next aisle, right about there." Leif pointed over the top of the cracker boxes with a thin, boney arm that matched his thin, boney frame. He was pretty tall for eleven, and wore dark rimmed glasses that really showed up against pale skin and his pencil straight hair, the color of snow.

Around the corner from Leif on the opposite aisle, Eric found eight clear plastic bins of whole coffee beans under hinged covers. He had no idea which coffee bin to choose, and he had no idea how much coffee in one bag made a pound.

"You look confused, pardner."

Eric looked up to see Mr. Anderlund, who carried a case of organic, canned soup.

The father was a taller, older version of his son.

" My mom forgot the coffee when she got groceries. Don't you have Folgers? That red package is the only one I know."

Mr. Anderlund put the box down on the floor, smiling. "Sorry, no Folgers. No Maxwell House, or Boyer's either. No ground coffee - just whole roasted beans in bulk."

At that moment Eric was really confused and decided this errand just to get some coffee, was really more complicated than it should be.

"Here, I'll measure out two pounds of our regular, medium roast, Columbian coffee. When your mom buys my whole beans, this is the coffee she usually gets."

Very relieved, Eric reached for a paper bag then opened it. "But she only asked for me to get one pound."

"One pound it is – more or less." Mr. Anderlund put in seven scoops of the coffee beans, weighed it then marked the price on the bag with a large wax pencil he kept tied to a string.

"Anything else?"

By then Eric just wanted to get back on his bike and go. He shook his head. "Nope. Just this."

"Okay, Mr. Molosky, I'll have you sign the accounts book to make this transaction official."

Mr. Anderlund put his arm around Eric's shoulder as they walked to the market's front counter. By the checkout till, a woman stood waiting with some fruit and organic snacks.

Eric didn't recognize this woman. She looked to be about as old as his brother's teacher, but certainly younger than his mother. She had short dark, wavy hair. Her skin and blue eyes were so pale her hair almost looked like a wig.

"Well," greeted Mr. Anderlund. "Hello, there. Are you new to Mosquito Creek or just visiting?" Mr. Anderlund was a very direct person and liked to know the details of any potential gossip, or as he called it "current events" firsthand. In fact, Mr. Anderlund was so current on so many town events and issues, the newspaper editor Mr. Sullivan, often called Mr. Anderlund for information.

The woman smiled. "Visiting, I guess. I'm here on business." She paid for the produce a bag of vegetable chips, then pulled out a business card. "Are you Carl Anderlund?"

Mr. Anderlund nodded. He was surprised but naturally very curious.

"I may need to speak with you later this week. This is my business card. My office and cell phone number are long distance, though I've noticed that my cell phone doesn't get reception so close to your mountains. No matter. To reach me locally you can leave a message with Sheriff Howard, or cottage number twelve at the Deer Lodge Motel."

She smiled at Mr. Anderlund, and to Eric then nodded to Leif who had watched everything from his vantage point on the top of the stepladder. The parakeets shrieked and the bell above the door rang as she opened it to return to her parked vehicle.

Mr. Anderlund watched her through the front window. Leif jumped to the floor from the step ladder and both boys rushed to look out the front screen door. The Jeep the lady drove had Iowa license plates. When Leif and Eric hurried back to the counter to ask about her business card, Mr. Anderlund was already on the phone. He handed the woman's card to Leif while he waited for the numbers he had pressed to connect.

> *Bella Perez, Claims Investigator*
> *Mid-Western Insurance*
> *1500 Mid-Western Tower*
> *Des Moines, Iowa*

Eric and Leif looked at each other, puzzled. They didn't know anyone from Des Moines and they didn't know anybody who knew anybody from Des Moines.

"Park hi, Carl here. How are you? Oh, I'm just fine." He motioned for Leif to return the business card and tapped it on the wooden counter top as he talked. "Say, there aren't any special events or seminars at the inn this coming week are there?"

The boys paid close attention to the end of the conversation they could hear.

The bell rang, the birds announced another customer and Eric's younger brother Marc skipped through the door followed by their grandpa, Gunther Molosky. Marc was much slimmer than his older brother with the same dark blonde hair as his mother.

Grandpa Molosky always looked serious. His dark brown eyes, thick brows, and straight, graying dark hair just added to his somber look.

The birds jumped from perch to perch in a flutter that sent even more small feathers to the floor, as Marc jumped around the cage tapping the mirror that hung above their water dish.

Calmly, Grandpa Molosky placed both of his large hands on his grandson's shoulders and steered him away from the agitated birds.

Eric, who as a general rule couldn't keep secrets anyway rushed to his grandpa and in a hushed voice - cause Mr. Anderlund was still on the phone—excitedly told him about the new stranger. "There was a detective here from Iowa. Where's Iowa? I forget."

Grandpa Molosky, not much impressed with modern education suspected that this time it wasn't the fault of the school. "You forget?"

Eric shrugged.

Leif arranged four boxes of wooden matches in the shape of an "L" then he pointed to each one in order whispering. "We're in Montana here, Wyoming is south of us, Nebraska is east of Wyoming and then Iowa is here, east of Nebraska."

Eric nodded that he understood.

Everyone waited while Mr. Anderlund was still talking on the phone.

"I see. I thought there might be a business conference... Oh, really? Have you spoken with Jeff? That figures. How about the Ranch are they talking? Okay. Uh huh. Sure will. Thanks, Park bye for now."

When Mr. Anderlund hung up he handed Mr. Molosky the business card the stranger had left without saying a word, quite unusual for him.

Eric's grandpa read the investigator's name, the name of the company and the out of state address then returned the card to Leif's father. "What's going on?"

Mr. Anderlund leaned forward on the counter. His long, thin body hung over the space like a draped coat. "This is p-r-e-t-t-y big stuff." He waved the business card in the air. "According to Park, who's writing a front page feature for next Friday's edition, this insurance investigator with Mid-Western arrived late yesterday. I didn't realize that Zara Grant disappeared seven years ago this coming August. And this...huh," Mr. Anderlund looked at the business card again. "Belinda Perez is here to complete a final investigation so the file can be closed and Zara Grant can be declared legally dead. Naturally Park is shaken but doing his job, just as he did when his granddaughter Zara disappeared."

Most of the kids in elementary and junior high now, were too young to remember the desperate, stormy night back in August 1990, when just about every adult in Mosquito Creek were out in a windy, cold rain, searching for the fourteen-year-old granddaughter of the local newspaper editor Park Sullivan and historic ranch owner, Khors Grant.

"There's eighteen thousand acres of ranch land and a huge fortune just sitting there. I expect that Zara's aunts, uncles and cousins have been crossing off the days–impatiently–waiting for these seven years to pass."

Grandpa Molosky look down at his two grandsons. "Not a word of this to your mother or your Aunt Monica. Especially your aunt, it's her twenty-first birthday today and she might not have heard anything yet. Your Aunt Monica and Zara Grant were best friends from first grade right through to grade nine. When Zara disappeared...Well...

Monica never completely got over the loss of her friend. Zara would have been twenty-one years-old as well later this month. Do I have your word, both of you?"

Eric and Marc nodded. "I promise, Grandpa." They pledged together.

CHAPTER THREE
The Questions Have Questions

June 12…

Grandpa Molosky loaded Eric's bike in the back of his truck and he and the boys rushed back to the house. Mr. Molosky had been worried about his daughter-in-law and her younger sister, while Eric had been worried about his Aunt Monica's birthday cake.

But the green cake, that only an hour before had looked more like garbage than dessert, was completely restored, on a clean plate in the middle of the kitchen table as if Joker had never happened. Eric was amazed. It looked great with no sign of its earlier close call with disaster.

Also in the kitchen and taped on the front of the fridge was a large piece of yellow lined paper that listed some chores for each of the three Molosky men. They dusted the living room, extend and set the dining table and then added more chairs. Grandpa Molosky moved the birthday cake safely to one end of the extended dining table and then they all stood back to check their work.

When the mantle clock on the dining room buffet chimed six o'clock, Marc got annoyed. "Where are the girls? How come they don't hav'ta help for Aunt Monica's birthday?"

The words were no sooner out of Marc's mouth when they heard the back screen door slam followed by both Sonia and Salina bursting through the swinging kitchen door into the dining room at the same time.

The Molosky sisters like their brothers were a split in family traits. Salina was Eric's fraternal twin. She had light brown curly hair kept in one single braid down her back. Sonia was slightly taller than her younger sister with shoulder length dark blonde hair like her mother and youngest brother Marc.

Both sisters tried to speak. They were almost out of breath. They choked and stammered in a stampede of words at the same time, with different information.

"Mom's at the hospital with Aunt Monica."

"Aunt Monica fainted."

"We gotta call everyone."

"We can't have the party tonight."

"Whoa, both of you." Grandpa Molosky held up a hand. "Take a deep breath."

Grandpa moved two dining chairs for his granddaughters and then he sat on a third one facing them. Eric and Marc stood on either side their grandpa watching their sisters.

"Sonia, from the top. First, how did you hear that Monica was at the hospital?"

"Mom called Mrs. McKenna. Salina and I were helping Gillian…."

Eric interrupted. "G-o-r-d-o-n."

"Shut up!" Salina snapped.

Eric hugged himself then made a kissing motion with his lips.

Marc burst out laughing.

"Eric!" Sonia started to get up from her chair.

Her grandpa stopped her then he looked at each of his four grandchildren. "Hey, folks…"

Grandpa Molosky was usually a steady brick of solid patience with them and all of their friends, but this time he wasn't in such a tolerant mood. "You're Aunt Monica - remember? Sonia continue."

"Mrs. McKenna talked to Mom then she came into the den." "Gillian, Salina and I were playing Scrabble." Sonia made a face at her brother.

"I thought you were sewing a skirt?" Eric interjected.

This time she ignored her brother and focused on her grandpa. "Mrs. McKenna said that Monica had fainted at the bank. Something about a strange woman in town asking questions. Someone at the bank called Mom. Then Mom met the ambulance at the hospital."

Grandpa Molosky nodded. He kept silent for a moment. After he read the business card at Anderlund's Market earlier, his first concern had been that Monica might hear about the insurance investigator before he had a chance to tell her.

"I need to get to the hospital to be with your mom and check on your aunt." Then he looked from Sonia, to Eric, to Salina, and Marc. "Is it possible for me to leave the four of you here, on your own without civil war breaking out?"

Everyone nodded. When Grandpa Molosky spoke even their friends listened.

"Good. Then, I'm off. Okay? And I'm sure by now that everyone in town has heard the news, so we won't likely have anyone showing up for cake. Oh, and since your mom obviously couldn't get dinner going, order a pizza."

"Cool." Marc ran for the kitchen phone. "I only like cheese. Can we order half and half?"

His grandfather followed him through the door. "Sure. Order a large. Half cheese, and half spinach!" Grandpa laughed as he disappeared out the back door.

"Spinach!" The older three made a face.

When the pizza arrived, Sonia had been reading while the younger kids watched the movie *Batman Returns*. With the box opened, the smell of the steam from the half cheese, half sausage pizza, made their mouths fill with saliva.

Sonia let everyone gather around the coffee table and sit on the floor to eat dinner with their hands. They put *Batman* on pause.

With a mouth full of cheese and pizza crust, Marc was curious. "How come Aunt Monica fainted? Is she real sick?"

"Not measles sick like you were in March." Sonia explained. "Mrs. McKenna said Aunt Monica's nerves have been bad ever since her best friend died."

Marc wanted to know more. "Who was Aunt Monica's best friend? How did she die? Was she sick?"

"Nobody knows how she died cause she just disappeared."

Sonia had turned eleven in early April and was the oldest of the four Molosky children. She was almost a full two years older than the twins, Salina and Eric, and three years older than Marc.

Sonia was only three and too young to remember the night Zara Grant disappeared. But she had been four and a half when her father Joe had not returned home the following October. Joe Molosky and his tow truck were nowhere to be found.

Two nights after her father disappeared, Sonia couldn't sleep and came downstairs looking for her mother. Though it was late she heard voices on the other side of the kitchen door. Her worried mother and grandpa were talking with Mr. Sullivan the newspaper editor, and his daughter Mrs. McKenna.

They talked about the night young Zara Grant disappeared, and the day Philip Peter's mother left town and they all thought it was peculiar how so many people from their small town just seemed to vanish.

Sonia returned to the present, then made a decision. She put down her half-eaten slice of pizza. "I'm going to share a huge secret with you." She looked at the faces of her sister and brothers with a very serious expression. "But you must swear not to share this secret with anyone, on pain of death."

This was another surprise turn of events, and there sure had been a lot of surprises on that day. All three of them nodded their agreement with a solemn expression.

"First, we have to go upstairs to Mom's room." Sonia stood and headed for the stairs. The others scrambled to follow.

The Molosky house was an older, storey and a half bungalow built in 1936. And because the pitched roof was low, the second floor had only two bedrooms and one small bathroom. The sisters and their mother slept upstairs. The boys shared the third bedroom on the main floor across the hall from their grandpa who had moved into the converted den permanently, after his son Joe didn't return.

Sonia stopped outside her mother's bedroom door. "Mom has another door at the back of her closet. I found it one day when she was out showing houses. I was trying on her new red sandals and kinda lost my balance."

Her brothers giggled and she scowled at them. "When I tried to keep from falling, what I thought was a wall was really a door and it just opened. There's a small handle, but it's painted the same color as the wall, so it's not easy to see. So follow me. Don't–touch anything! Got that?"

All three nodded again without saying a word.

In single file they followed Sonia into their mother's bedroom. They watched as Sonia push the hanging clothes first left, then right, to reveal a hidden door only four feet high, at the back of the long closet.

Sonia opened the door and felt around for the string she had discovered earlier that morning attached to one light bulb. With more light they could see the attic space was an unfinished area only eight feet long and six feet wide. The floor was unpainted plywood. They could see the pointed ends of nails that came through the pine planks underneath the roof shingles outside. The small space was hot and smelled musty.

Sonia pointed. "Those cardboard boxes are packed with dad's clothes, his business papers, his pictures and other stuff. In that blue suitcase are Mom's keepsakes and stuff. But this gray suitcase belongs to Aunt Monica. It has all kinds of information and newspaper clippings, a bunch of photographs and history stuff about her friend, Zara Grant."

Eric spoke up. "The Grant Ranch, Zara Grant?"

Sonia nodded. "That's the one. Zara Grant's dad and mom were killed in a car accident when Zara was three. Her grandfather was a widower and he pretty well raised his granddaughter with the help of his sister, Mrs. Knudsen."

"And Zara Grant was the only one who would have inherited not just the ranch from her grandfather, but all the money from oil wells and mining too. We're talking millions and millions and millions of dollars."

Their faces showed surprise, but Salina, Marc and Eric stood perfectly silent.

Sonia almost reclosed the door then made a decision. She picked up the small gray suitcase and wiped off more dust. "We better get outta here. I'll put this under my bed for now."

Salina was instantly alarmed. "Seriously, have you lost your mind? Mom may go looking for that again, especially now!"

Sonia hesitated then kept the suitcase and closed the short door. "It's pretty dusty all over in there and it doesn't look like Mom's been in the closet for quite a while. With that insurance lady in town…she might look…or not."

Like a line of ducks the kids filed out through the closet door into their mother's bedroom. Sonia stopped for a moment by the ironing board considering the grey suitcase one more time then decided that what she planned to do was worth the risk.

She wiped the dust off her hands then pulled her mother's clothing together to fill the space on the rod that hid the attic door. Back across the hall the younger kids sat on Salina's bed in the room the girls shared. They watched Sonia push the suitcase under her bed then as she stood at the doorway to make sure the swiped luggage couldn't be seen from the open bedroom door.

Eric was curious. "So with Zara gone, who gets the ranch and all the money, Aunt Monica?"

Sonia sat on the edge of her bed facing them. "No of course not. Mr. Grant's sister gets everything. That would be Mrs. Knudsen, and her two horrible sons, and their equally nasty wives, and all those spoiled grandchildren, like Anna."

All the Molosky kids knew the youngest of those spoiled grandchildren. Anna Knudsen was twelve and as far as Sonia was concerned the most irritating of the five Knudsen grandchildren.

Mrs. Knudsen moved to Mosquito Creek originally to help her brother with the Inn and Zara. But two months after her brother died Mrs. Knudsen's two sons, their wives and children showed up and then moved right in to live at the historic ranch as if they were the original settlers. Everyone in town was annoyed by their attitude.

Sonia could hardly wait to dig a little further into what happened to her Aunt Monica's best friend. "Zara Grant just vanished. No trace of her was ever found which, is a true mystery."

She decided to wait another day to re-inspect the suitcase. But Sonia had questions and knew she'd need lots of help with finding how some of those questions could be answered.

The dining room clock chimed eight.

Always the big sister, Sonia took charge again. "We better finish our pizza and then get into our pajamas before Mom or Grandpa come home."

CHAPTER FOUR
The Race Is On

June 13…

Zara Grant's disappearance was a real life unsolved mystery and Sonia had decided that for her Aunt Monica's twenty-first birthday, as maybe a kind of present, she would try to find out what happened to her aunt's childhood friend. But she wasn't in much of a mood to race with the others so she watched Mia Cho take her turn as the race-starter and time keeper.

"R-e-a-d-y… Set… Go!" Mia waved the black and white checkered shirt Sonia pilfered from Grandpa Molosky's laundry hamper.

Tires spun and the racers were off for the first race of summer vacation. Sonia and Mia stepped back as one by one ten cyclists went airborne over a steep, nine-foot drop to the narrow dirt road below.

Like a bunch of bees on bicycles, the group swarmed down the hill then disappeared from their sight. The girls had to shield their eyes from dust the spinning tires stirred up high above their heads.

Over the past two summers the race distance had gotten longer to almost three-quarters of a mile. The new starting point was from the top of the ridge that overlooked Lost Creek. From that ridge the official race path followed along the edge of the creek to below the train trestle bridge at Bitter Root Crossing.

When the last cyclist disappeared, Mia and Sonia slid down the side of the hill to take a short cut through the trees to the race finish.

As usual Stephen Anderlund and Gordon McKenna were the race leaders.

From the ridge they had launched their bikes skyward. With plenty of air they never touched the dirt road below.

They landed, peddling stroke-for-stroke straight through the wild oats that grew beside it.

Wild oats grew at the top of a shorter six-foot drop through low scrub brush and buffalo grass to the edge of Lost Creek where a narrow deer path took a sharp turn to the right.

All the competitors knew that it was real important to reach that deer path first. Cause the racer who reached the deer path first could keep the lead for most of the race before there was any place wide enough for anyone else to pass or try to make a break for the finish.

Gordon twisted his handlebars sharply to the right steering blindly through the branches of a tall willow bush and creating his own bit of a shortcut. He almost over shot the deer path when it twisted sharply to the left and then right again.

Stephen pushed hard to catch up so his front tire was right behind Gordon's back fender by the time the path dipped down to a narrow "V" then up again, and over a bunch of bumpy tree roots.

Everyone was a year older, slightly taller and much stronger so it looked like this race was going to break last summer's time record. The distance between the leaders and Bitter Creek Crossing was shrinking fast.

Gordon and Stephen were sixty feet and closing from a place where the deer path got wider. He knew that Stephen would make his move as soon as they got to that point so, Gordon got ready for his own burst of speed.

Only eleven feet before that very point grew eight large birch trees on the right side of the trail. And in no more time than it takes to blink, Stephen had a new idea for his own shortcut. In a gutsy, bold move, he abruptly jerked his handlebars sending his bike off the path into tall grass and straight for two of the birch trees.

There was only a narrow space between one tree rooted at the edge of the path and the second tree that grew barely two feet away from it. And in that split moment – Stephen also realized if he didn't ride between those two trees with his bike perfectly straight up, he would hit one or both of those very hard trunks.

Leif Anderlund and Joey Salas were chasing the leaders with a back to front race of their own. As they came around a short blind curve the challengers realized they were just twelve feet behind Gordon and Stephen. Leif saw his older brother make the move first. Then Joey spotted Stephen. Startled, their jaws dropped and they actually forgot to keep peddling.

Gordon's back was to everyone else with all his concentration on skidding to his victory stop at the train bridge.

In a flash, Stephen shot between both ash trees. With his feet still a blur he peddled right over a small juniper bush and popped back onto the deer path exactly a yard ahead of Gordon – in a full out dash.

Startled, Gordon's feet stopped pushing. He checked over his right shoulder. Then he looked behind completely rattled. "What...? How?" Then he braked to a complete stop. He had too, he was laughing too hard to peddle.

The other racers caught up to Gordon. He still smiled and shook his head. "Man that was a cool move. Kinda stupid, but real cool."

"Kinda stupid? Are you kidding me!" Hanna Gaikis, the same age as Stephen and Gordon, was shaken by the near-miss. "If Stephen had hit those trees, every single one of his bones woulda been oh so broken!"

When everyone crossed the official finish line, even with the risk, everyone was pretty impressed with Stephen Anderlund's smooth move.

Waiting with Stephen below the train bridge, was Mia and Sonia a little out of breath in spite of the short cut.

26

Before Sonia had found the grey suitcase - bike races, scavenger hunts, swimming on hot days, and thinking of Gordon McKenna, were most of her thoughts for most of the summer weeks - but the grey suitcase and the arrival of the insurance lady changed everything.

Sonia couldn't seem to get her Aunt Monica's missing childhood friend of out of her mind. But she knew she'd need a lot of help to find evidence against the rude Knudsen family and to do that she had her own important childhood friends that she somehow needed to convince to join in with her.

CHAPTER FIVE
Back In Time

June 14...

"Aren't they ever going to leave!" Sonia jumped up from the living room chair again. Since their late breakfast she'd been in and out of it a dozen times, upstairs then back down, at least four times. Her sister and brothers had stopped paying any attention to her and just watched their movie.

It was late the previous night when Sonia heard her mother and her grandpa come home with her Aunt Monica. Monica slept in Mrs. Molosky's room and didn't wake up until half way through the morning.

From the kitchen the kids heard muffled sobs and then hushed conversation, when the scenes of *Superman II* didn't have something exploding.

With a flash light, in the dark, at the end of her bed Sonia had rummaged through some of the papers again the night before and was even more certain there was a clue to the mystery of Zara Grant's disappearance, somewhere in the grey suitcase she had taken from her mother's closet.

When she told Mia and Hanna, they were instantly excited by the thought of a real mystery and clues hidden in the snitched luggage, stashed under Sonia's bed. Naturally they were relieved because it wasn't under their bed and they weren't the ones who would be grounded for all eternity if it was discovered.

But after the bike race it wasn't so easy to get Joey, Leif and his older brother Stephen to pay much attention. At first they had been real skeptics. But they usually followed Gordon's lead. And when the boys finished reliving the bike race, for the third time, Gordon had shown some curiosity.

He didn't remember his cousin Zara very well but Gordon was completely devoted to his grandfather Park Sullivan. He would do anything to make his grandfather proud.

Because Sonia hardly slept all night and she fretted that her mother would discover what she had done. She was very tired and very jumpy – so she paced. As she paced, she watched the closed kitchen door.

She decided that waiting her turn to see the dentist was easier than this. Sonia felt stuck. How could she meet her friends while the adults were all still home? The grey suitcase certainly couldn't leave the house. At breakfast, her mother had asked her to stay home to watch her younger sister and brothers, so why weren't they gone?

In her mind she changed her original plan. Her secret team could still meet in the Molosky's garage at noon but they couldn't cycle to Lost Creek, they'd have to stay there. Most of her friends were in a time crunch that day.

Stephen Anderlund had promised to work for his dad at the store after lunch. Mia Cho had to work at her mother's flower shop then too. Joey Salas was needed at his grandparent's restaurant to help clean up and Hanna Gaikas was supposed to look after Mrs. Carter's twins. Leif Anderlund and Gordon McKenna were the only two members of the group who had the afternoon free.

The clock struck the half hour. It was eleven-thirty and still none of the adults seemed ready to leave. Sonia was antsy and kept pacing around the dining table. She wondered if she should cancel the garage meeting? Or, should she let everyone show up as if they were just getting together for a visit? She was in such a stew she thought her head would explode.

Marc walked passed her heading for the kitchen door.

"Where're you going?" Sonia snapped.

"I want some juice." Marc stepped out of range in case she sung at him. "A guy gets thirsty once in a while." He made a face as he backed closer to the kitchen door.

"Don't–you–say–anything." She waved her finger at him. Earlier Marc almost gave her plans away - twice - before Sonia distracted him and the twins with the movie. "But find out if they're still going to meet with Mr. Sullivan at the newspaper?"

"You just told me...*not-to-say-anything.*" He mimicked her gestures.

"Oh how I envy Hanna Gaikis. She's an only child! You little chunk of dried snot – you know what I meant."

"How could I? I'm a little-chunk-of-dried-snot. That makes *you* a *BIG* chunk of dried snot!" He giggled. "You wanna know, you ask." Marc shouldered the edge of the hinged door and it swung open.

Sonia caught just a glimpse. Her aunt's back was to the open door. Her mother stood at the sink rinsing out a coffee mug. Joker, their four-footed vacuum sat at his usual post under the kitchen table waiting for any stuff to drop. Grandpa grabbed Marc and in one swift motion flipped him upside down and tickled his belly.

The door swung back toward the dining room. Sonia heard her brother laughing while he objected. "Let me go."

Still torn about what to do, Sonia spotted Mia, Joey and Leif cycle passed the dining room window on the driveway. She panicked. They were fifteen minutes early! In a bee's blink she was out the front door, cleared the front porch, and sprinted to the side driveway.

Between gulps of air Sonia whispered. "They're - still - here." She pointed to the closed garage door. After one deep breath she found she could talk and breathe at the same time. "I don't know - when they're going to the newspaper. My aunt Monica is..."

"Hi Mrs. Molosky." Leif spotted Sonia's mother at the back porch door.

"Leif, Mia, Joey. How are you?" Mrs. Molosky greeted the familiar faces.

"Fine." They said in sync.

Ursula Molosky looked at the bikes then back to the kids. "What are your plans or the day?"

"Scavenger hunt." Sonia blurted. "We're planning another scavenger hunt."

Mrs. Molosky sighed. "That actually sounds like fun." She wished she was twelve, again. "But don't forget your brothers they eat like locusts. Make sure they have at least one piece of fruit with their lunch and not just chips all day. We're leaving in a few minutes"

"Okay Mom."

Sonia's mother left the back porch, screen door then disappeared back into the house.

"Why do I always feel like I just knocked a baby bird from a nest when I lie to my mother?" Sonia felt a little nauseous and guilty. Except for a little help from her grandpa, her mother was alone raising four kids, running her own real estate business and now, her younger sister had moved in and was falling apart.

"You can put your bikes over by the fence, right there." Sonia pointed to the space between the garage and the carport where Grandpa Molosky parked his 1965, half-ton pickup truck.

"T-e-c-h-n-i-c-a-l-l-y," offered Joey. "What you told your mom wasn't a lie."

Mia got it. "That's right. We're looking for clues to Zara Grant's disappearance." She shrugged. "That's *like* a scavenger hunt."

31

Hanna arrived and stopped her bike. "What's like a scavenger hunt…?"

But they all turned to the sound of loud voices. Stephen and Gordon were racing each other again. They made the sharp turn onto the entrance of the driveway with Gordon in the lead by just his front wheel. Laughing they breezed by the five onlookers standing at the edge of the brick drive.

Cycling too fast and with no space left to stop – the boys parted in a "V". Gordon headed to the left into the back yard and Stephen skidded to the right, across the gravel between the garage and the parked truck.

As Gordon and Stephen pushed their bikes back to where the others stood, the garage door opened. They turned to see Grandpa Molosky. He stood on the bottom step of the back porch with the garage door opener in one hand and the keys to the mini-van in the other. He had seen the end of the race.

"You two are both twelve?"

"Yes sir." Gordon and Stephen answered. They couldn't tell if Mr. Molosky was angry or just mildly annoyed.

"Hmm." Grandpa Molosky headed for the open garage door. "Well, I guess that gives me a full four years before I need to fear for my life with you two behind the wheel of something that has a motor."

Gordon and Stephen still couldn't tell. They looked at Sonia. Sonia shook her head and shrugged.

Grandpa Molosky got into the van, backed it out of the garage and stopped part way down the driveway at the edge of the front sidewalk. Mrs. Molosky and her sister Monica, both wore sunglasses as they stepped into the van. In the street Grandpa pointed the vehicle north toward main street and Mr. Sullivan's newspaper office.

"They're gone!" Marc leaped from behind the cottonwood that grew next to the driveway, in the front yard. He ran to his sister, bare foot and still in pajamas. "I saw them turn the corner. Sonia, can we have ice cream for lunch?"

32

With a deep sigh, she checked her watch. It was noon, exactly. "Y-e-s." She hoped the ice cream would buy his silence. She turned to the others. "Get yourself a lawn chair. It'll be shady in the garage. I'll be back in a minute." She followed her brother into the house.

"Okay, go get Eric and Salina." In the kitchen she lined up three bowls with three spoons then retrieved the bucket of vanilla flavored ice cream from the freezer. All three of the younger kids came running through the swinging door at the same time. With a thump and scrape of three chairs they were seated.

"Do you want sliced peaches or sliced bananas on your ice cream?"

"Chocolate sauce." Eric spoke up.

"Mom gave me specific orders that you had to eat some fruit with your lunch." She looked at each of them impatient.

They shrugged.

"Sliced bananas it is."

All three nodded. Hurriedly Sonia filled soup bowls with lots of ice cream topped with bananas for each of them. With their mouths busy, she raced up stairs to the bedroom she shared with her sister. From under her bed Sonia pulled out the grey suit case.

She rushed back to the garage taking the front door. She already regretted sharing so much information with her younger siblings. She knew better. When her brothers got excited they talked too much. Her sister was a little better at keeping a secret but still a risk.

With the suitcase open on the floor of the garage, Sonia showed her friends the front page of the local paper dated almost seven years before. She read the front page story out loud. When she finished she passed it to Mia who looked at the photos before she passed it to Joey who passed it to Hanna. The paper went around to everyone.

THE MOSQUITO CREEK WEEKLY REVIEW   August 18, 1990
Mosquito Creek, Montana   Park Sullivan, Editor

...LOCAL GIRL GOES MISSING IN SEVERE STORM...

Sometime in the late evening of August 16, my fourteen year-old granddaughter Zara Grant, vanished.

Zara Grant is heiress to a vast, historic, family fortune. Her paternal grandfather Kohrs Grant reported her missing to local authorities. Mr. Grant became concerned when about an hour after Zara left her home at Grant Ranch to go riding, her horse returned to the ranch alone.

An immediate search for the teenager was hampered by a severe rainstorm that moved into the area with over 100 recorded lighting strikes throughout the night.

Sheriff, Jeff Howard, was interviewed by The Review. The sheriff stated that he did not suspect foul play as they expected to find Zara with the help of local tracking dogs. "That storm rolled in pretty fast." The Sheriff stated. "Her horse likely threw her and she is just hurt, maybe has a broken leg."

As the search for Zara progresses the Review will keep Powell County residents informed.

Just below the text was a photograph of Zara Grant. She sat on her prize winning Quarter Horse, Butterscotch. The broad smile of the freckled faced red head looked right at the camera. She held the reins of her horse in her left hand and the blue ribbon for barrel racing in her right hand.

Gordon was only five and a half when his cousin disappeared. Over time pictures of Zara had been put away in his home and at his grandparents'. He had forgotten what Zara looked like. But as he studied the image, even though part of her face was shadowed by the brim of her cowboy hat, she looked like a younger copy of his own mother.

His friends watched quietly as Gordon looked at the newspaper picture of the cousin he missed knowing. Then he abruptly looked up from the front page. "I think I have a clue, or a point, or

34

something…maybe. If Zara and Butterscotch won barrel races for heaven's sake, then her getting thrown from her horse – any horse, would be slim. And another thing, well trained ranch horses don't spook that easy. Not even in a storm."

Stephen jumped in. "You think Sheriff Howard missed that fact or do you think he suspected foul play, but didn't want to say it?"

"We'd hav'ta ask him that." Sonia offered. "But not just yet. For now we're planning one of our scavenger hunts – if anyone asks."

"Oh that's what you were talking about when I arrived." Hanna nodded. "That's a great idea."

Mia, always organized, opened a bright pink backpack she brought with her. She took out a lined notebook and pen. "We better make some notes guys, or we won't get anywhere." She began to write. "So, our first question we need to answer is: do we think this was an accident or foul play?

Gordon spoke first. "Our poking around may show otherwise but I vote foul play."

Mia took a count. "Who else thinks this was foul play?"

Everyone raised their hand. "Okay, based on Gordon's first observation with Zara Grant's riding ability and her horse's training – we agree that we're looking for clues to a crime."

Mia wrote the results of the vote then she made another note. "If we agree it was foul play then there needs to be a motive."

Hanna spoke up. "That's easy, money."

"That's too easy." Joey was skeptical.

"But logical." Gordon argued. "She was only fourteen but she was an heiress to millions of dollars in oil, cattle and real estate." He looked at each face in the circle. "I overheard my folks talking."

"That's not just talk." Sonia reached for a 1989 *Time Magazine*. "There's a lot of Grant Ranch information written in here too."

35

Stephen, always logical, shook his head. "But wait a minute. Zara's disappearance could easily have been an accident. When she went missing, she hadn't inherited anything. Her grandfather was healthy and alive."

"Then he died," Joey held up another front page in his hands. "Two months later of a heart attack."

"Be careful with those papers." Sonia cautioned. "I don't want my mother to think the stuff in this suitcase has been disturbed."

"Exactly." Stephen started to confuse even himself. "Heart attacks are a very natural way to die. If Zara was murdered for money then Mr. Grant had to be murdered and for the same reason. That's two murders in two months! And, except for a possible gunfight about a hundred years ago - when has Mosquito Creek had any real crime?"

Stephen looked at Mia. "I think I might want to change my vote."

Everyone suddenly looked just as bewildered, except Sonia and Gordon.

Sonia pitched her theory. "We see news stories all the time where surprises happen – even crime in small towns. Who gains from having Zara and her grandfather out of the way?" She looked at each of her friends. "Zigvarta Knudsen - Mr. Grant's skuzzy sister and her equally vile sons, their wives and their kids."

Leif nearly tipped over his lawn chair when he jumped up. "Hold it." He looked at Gordon. "You're Zara's cousin. Do you inherit anything?"

"What! Gordon shook his head. "What are you saying?"

Stephen tugged on Leif's sleeve and motioned for his younger brother to sit down. "Now we're really off track. No one inherits anything unless someone leaves them something in their will. Mr. Grant obviously changed his will after Zara disappeared."

Mia jumped up. "Wait Leif could be right. If Mrs. Knudsen and her son's are found responsible for Zara's disappearance, which then contributed to Mr. Grant's heart attack, the estate would go to Zara's maternal aunt…Gordon's mother."

The sudden silence filled the entire garage.

Leif was the first to move. He folded his arms with a smug smile on his face.

Hanna checked her watch. "I hav'ta go. But really this could get very, very dangerous."

Hanna retrieved her bike then walked with it part way into the garage. "If Mrs. Knudsen, or her son's went to all the risk and all the trouble of bumping off two family members so they could get Grant Ranch and the rest of the estate – they would sure murder again. And after waiting seven years, they really want that investigator to declare Zara Grant legally dead and close the file."

In somber silence the six remaining friends watched Hanna peddle away.

Joey spoke first. He took Mia's notes from her lap then he turned the note pad toward the group. "I'm no lawyer yet, but look at this. Here's Mr. Grant, who lost his son and changed his will for his granddaughter. But if none of the other relatives could inherit the ranch until now, doesn't than mean Mr. Grant didn't redo his will after Zara went missing?"

Mia rechecked her list of deceased Grant family names. "Joey's right! Wow, that must have been a nasty surprise. No wonder Mrs. Knudsen's been cranky all these years."

"Speaking of cranky. Hanna's right too." Leif pointed down at the open suitcase. This could be huge if our poking around starts to look like there was two murders and not just two accidents."

Leif looked at Sonia. "We're gonna need to look at these papers again, many times. Can't we take this stuff somewhere and keep it to see it again?"

"No!" Sonia was so shaken she got the hic-ups. "I can't - *hic* - risk my mother – *hic* - missing this." She held her breath then swallowed. "She'll ask *me* first."

Joey held up the first finger of his right hand. They all knew this was a signal that he just had an great idea. "We could make copies of all the papers in this suitcase. Then after, you just return it with all its' stuff right back to your mother's closet."

"You mean we should make notes from the stuff here?" Mia asked.

Stephen jumped in. "No. Not hand written notes, photocopies. That's a great idea, Joey." He turned to Gordon. "The rest of us have to be somewhere else in a few minutes. But you and my brother could use the copier at your grandfather's newspaper this afternoon. Make the copies. Bring the suitcase back to Sonia and she returns it to her mother's closet. We have a duplicate. We're set."

"Here." Mia offered. "Take my backpack. We can keep the copies in it with my notes."

"Making copies could be a little tricky." Sonia reminded them. "My mother, grandpa and my aunt were meeting with the sheriff, Gordon's parents and grandparents – at – the newspaper office this afternoon."

Gordon looked at Leif. "We can wait a little and make copies later this afternoon when everyone's gone. If not, then we may have to make them tonight."

Her heart felt like it was thumping in the back of her throat. She expected the plan to copy everything, to go very wrong. But Sonia watched with fingers crossed, as Gordon and Leif peddled away with her mother's grey suitcase swinging by the grip of
Gordon's left handlebar.

CHAPTER SIX
The Best Fishing Hole

June 15…

That morning both Anderlund boys were on duty at the market. Their dad had taped a brown paper bag to the till with each chore printed in large block letters. Stephen read from the list of tasks out loud.

"One: the front windows need to be washed. Two: the floor must be swept. Three: the potato bin refilled. Four: the vitamin isle restocked. Five: the…"

Leif wasn't patient. "Why don't ya just cut the bag in half? I'll take some and you take some. You – read – so – slow. I'm gonna be another year older!"

"Well at least I can read donkey-feet." Stephen pulled himself up, over the top of the counter and had to stretch to reach the scissors that hung from hook just below the cash drawer. With one snip the bottom half of the paper bag list landed on the floor.

"That's your half." He pointed to the floor grinning at his younger brother. "I'll get my bucket and sponges."

Leif had been real jittery. He wanted to get his chores done early so he could meet Gordon behind the newspaper office right after lunch that afternoon.

Gordon still had the grey suitcase, cause they hadn't been able to make any copies the day before. They hung around a full hour waiting for the meeting between Gordon's family and Sonia's family to get over.

And then they watched in complete disbelief as Mr. Sullivan locked the side door of the newspaper when he left. No one in Mosquito Creek ever locked any doors, cars, houses, offices…nothing.

Gordon and Leif were left with two predicaments. The first, was a safe hiding place for Mrs. Molosky's grey suitcase. The second, was explaining to Sonia that wouldn't cause her cardiac arrest, why she couldn't have the suitcase back – quite, yet.

As Leif quickly scanned his half of the chore list, his eyes stopped at the task that was second last. "Hey, no way."

Stephen walked passed his brother heading for the front door carrying window washing supplies.

"You stuck me with the bird cage!" Leif complained to the back of his departing brother. "Those birds hate me. I'll be pecked to death."

Stephen let the screen door slam behind him.

Leif ran after him. "I'll trade ya the windows for the bird's cage."

"Nope." Stephen soaped down a tall narrow window at the far end of the platform. "That's what ya get for being a snot. You wouldn't let me finish reading the list…I–read–so–slow…remember?"

"You fly-vomit!" Leif stomped back into the store through the grocery section to the storage room by the loading dock. The boys' new stepsister Heather was working with her mother in the back. Their stepmother had received several boxes shipped from New Mexico.

In the dozens of boxes were one hundred and twelve red-clay pots, vases and jars of varying shapes and sizes. In two other shipments that also arrived the same week as the pots, were eighteen boxes of silk and dried flowers.

The back of the store looked like a small scale city of cardboard skyscrapers that towered none too well above everyone's head.

Heather looked up from pulling shredded packing paper from the top of yet another box. She had the same dazed expression on her face that Dr. Howes' cat had when he climbed out of the mayor's rain barrel. Her mother had dozens of complicated designs of mixed silk with naturally dried flowers, arranged in the clay pots and vases to sell at their reserved rodeo grounds booth.

The Grant Ranch Roundup was every year just one week before The Calgary Stampede. The cowboys competed in the Rodeo Prize Money Circuit around Texas and Oklahoma then traveled to Montana. After Montana the cowboys headed for Alberta, Canada then back to Wyoming, for Cheyenne Frontier Days.

Leif knew his stepmother had just a week to finish all seventy-five floral displays before the historic Grant Ranch Roundup began. When he heard her give Heather orders her voice was strained as tight as a violin string. As he hurried by to get a garbage bag, to tackle the dreaded birdcage, Leif got an idea.

"Heather why don't you let me help pack and move the boxes of finished pots. Those look heavy. I'll let you clean out the birds' cage. Penny and Nickel like you."

Heather looked pleadingly at her mother. "Is that alright?"

Mrs. Anderlund was only half listening to the kids. "What?"

"I'll help you pack and lift those boxes." Leif offered. "If you can spare Heather for a few minutes. She can clean the bird cage."

"Oh I hate those birds." Mrs. Anderlund hissed. "They're so messy. They're noisy. For goodness sake Heather, wear gloves. Leif, you can take that box by the door. It's ready to go out. Mr. Molosky let me borrow his truck while your dad is out."

At first, Leif was majorly relieved that he didn't have to deal with Penny and Nickel. But his stepmother proved only slightly less irritating than cleaning the bird cage.

As Leif carried a second box of finished arrangements out to Grandpa Molosky's parked truck, he understood why his dad had opted to make the rounds that morning of the green houses to replenish store supplies of fresh herbs.

Then Leif's plan went south. He had just pushed the third box into the front corner by the second box when he heard several high-pitched shrieks. Then he heard Heather scream his name. "Leif!" followed by the sound of tumbling boxes and then a lower pitched wail, followed by some serious swearing by his stepmother.

When his stepmother streaked, "Leif…!" "Stephen…!" Leif took a giant leap from the back of the truck to the loading dock and sprinted through the open shipping door.

In the back of the store that had once been a baggage area for the train station, his stepmother shuffled back and forth across the length of an antique harvest table, wildly waving a broom at the airborne parakeet, Nickel.

One tower of unpacked boxes had already toppled as the frantic bird flew from the top of a box, to a light fixture, to the top of a shelf and then on to a second light.

"Look what that filthy trouble maker has done!"

Leif didn't realize that human vocal cords could reach that high.

Heather stood at the end of the canned soup isle wearing the yellow rubber gloves that went passed her elbows. "I'm sorry." Tears dripped off her chin. "I don't know what happened. Penny stayed on her perch, but Nickel flew right at me when I opened the door!"

Mrs. Anderlund had a streak of bird droppings down her left arm. There was another blob on the table and a third splotch that had landed on a finished flower arrangement.

Leif was sure he'd need to escape to Norway. His stepmother was so crazed, he expected her to turn green and burst out of her tank top like the *Hulk*.

"Everyone stay still." Stephen took charge. "I'll get some blue berries. Nickel really likes blue berries. He turned around and almost collided with his father.

Mr. Anderlund had just returned. He carried a flat cardboard box of small plant pots of fresh parsley, basil, thyme and oregano. Nickel took off from the top of a vitamin sign and landed on Mr. Anderlund's head.

"What-is-going-on-here?" Mr. Anderlund's stone, grey expression was directed to everyone in his family…who in turn…looked at Leif.

****

Stephen finished his lunch then peddled off to meet Gordon at the newspaper. Leif was grounded. And part of his punishment was to finish every task on the list his father had left for both his sons as well as help his stepmother with her clay pots and vases.

Gordon was surprised to see Stephen. "Where's Leif? I thought you had to work."

"My brilliant brother is grounded for a week with extra chores." Stephen related the escaped bird incident. He painted a gritty picture of the scene that had greeted his father. "It was one of those treasured family moments."

Stephen gestured in the air. "My new stepmother was standing on that long table she has in the back. She had bird poop down one arm and was waving a broom at Nickel with the other but all she managed to hit was a stack of unpacked boxes and break a light bulb. Heather was hysterical. She was crying and still wearing those huge, yellow rubber gloves that went almost up to her shoulders."

Gordon wiped tears of laughter from his cheeks, shaking his head. "Poor Leif. Heather's mother was always a tough teacher, real quick to dump on the detention. Man! Now she's your mom!"

Stephen made a face. "I try not to think about it. What's the plan?"

"If I don't get this suitcase back to Sonia and soon, her skin's gonna drop off – she's one giant, raw nerve. Fortunately, my grandfather's leavin soon to go fishin' with Sonia's grandpa. We won't have time to read anything – just copy everything and then go through it later."

Gordon pretended to clean and organize the dark room until his grandfather left. As soon as his van disappeared around the corner, the boys got to work. Stephen carefully removed any staples and smoothed out folds in the originals, while Gordon made the copies.

****

Sonia brought her bike to a stop at the bottom of the platform steps. Leif was sweeping. "What are you doing here?" She suddenly had some difficulty breathing.

"Shouldn't you be helping Gordon make photocopies? That entire suitcase should be back in my mom's closet!" She took a deep breath. "If my mom goes looking for it to help out that insurance lady, I'll have to change my name and move to Canada!"

"Or, you can move to Norway with me."

"What?" Sonia scowled.

"I'm grounded."

"What!" She was light headed again.

"Don't get your toes in a knot. Stephen met Gordon in my place. That's all I know." He leaned on the handle of the broom.

Sonia's heart rate began to return to normal "I don't want a gathering at the house again so I thought we could meet at Lost Creek. If we take our fishing poles no one will see us doin anything unusual. But we need everybody."

Sonia persisted. "There was no answer at Hanna's. Do you know if she's baby sitting today or where she might be?"

44

Leif wondered why she asked him. Had she found out his brother had a crush on Hanna? Leif didn't think anyone else suspected. He began to push the broom again. "I don't know. She babysat all most all last week for Mrs. Carter. But I haven't seen Hanna today. If her mom's working at the café – she'd know."

Sonia pointed her bike in the direction of town. She hoped that if she hurried she might be able to catch Gordon and Stephen at the newspaper office, get her mother's suitcase back...then...she needed to find Hanna.

The Tumbleweed Café faced Grant Street. It was impossible to miss. The sign was long, narrow and covered the entire length of the building's front roof line. Painted across the sign were pink pigs pulling a covered wagon. The wagon was filled with black and white chickens, on a road flanked by tumbleweeds. A painted three-foot mug of coffee was at the end of the sign, just above the door.

Hanna's mother, Susan Gaikis, waited tables at the Tumbleweed Café. For extra money Mrs. Gaikis often picked up other shifts at the steak house next door, the Rocky Mountain *Hoof* .

From the street you couldn't tell that both restaurants were connected. The front door of the *Hoof* faced Bitter Root Avenue. The two restaurants were joined by two business owners who had two entirely different approaches to food.

Mrs. Jean Carter ran the Tumbleweed Café. The café served breakfast and lunch on flowered print table cloths with matching cloth napkins. On her menu were crepes and finger sandwiches with the crusts neatly cut off.

Mr. Gene Carter ran the *Hoof.* He was a former rodeo competitor who opened his restaurant, furnished with unpainted, pine picnic style tables. The floor was slate stone, almost always covered by discarded peanut shells. Mr. Carter's idea of an appetizer was a small aluminum bucket filled with peanuts, at each table for customers to munch while they waited for their steak. The *Hoof* served happy hour and dinner.

As it was still too early for the *Hoof* to be open, Sonia peeked inside the door of the Tumbleweed. Mrs. Carter was at the front till that was on a converted antique buffet.

As usual, Mrs. Carter's hair was perfectly styled, with several layers of wind-proof hair spray. Her blouse and ankle length skirt were so crisply starched and pressed it looked as if they were ironed while she wore them.

Sonia thought Mrs. Carter was a snob. She acted like she was elected '*Boss* of the world'. But Sonia needed to speak with Hanna's mother and there was no getting passed Mrs. Carter.

"Your grandfather is over there having coffee with Mr. Sullivan." Mrs. Carter almost coughed the word, "coffee". That was all Grandpa Molosky ever ordered in her restaurant. Grandpa Molosky said that Mrs. Carter charged far too much for "a darn egg" and that she was, "just a little too full of herself".

"Thank you Mrs. Carter but I wasn't here to see my grandpa. I just had a question for Mrs. Gaikis."

Mrs. Carter came around the end of the buffet counter. "Mrs. Gaikis is working and not due for her break for another forty-three minutes. You can either wait, or perhaps I can deliver a message for you."

Sonia didn't understand why there were some people a person couldn't wait to see again and again – while there were other people, a person really never wanted to see even once. So, if Mrs. Carter moved to somewhere far, far away...like France...Sonia knew she'd feel sorry for France. "I guess all I needed to ask Mrs. Gaikis, was if Hanna was babysitting today? There was no answer at their apartment"

"Yes she is and do not even think of going to my home. My twins maybe four now but they still need a great deal of attention. Hanna cannot be distracted."

"Oh no, of course not Mrs. Carter. I was only asking because a bunch of us were going fishing and I thought Hanna might like to join us."

"Not today, or much of this week either..." Mrs. Carter's attention was diverted by a new waitress who carried a very large tray at a very dangerous angle. The café owner rushed away to rescue the edge of the tray from hitting one of her seated guests in the head.

Sonia backed away to the door and the parting scene before she fled, was of Mrs. Carter gesturing with both arms in the air, as she lectured the new wait staff.

Back outside, Sonia relaxed and got her bike. She checked through one of the small panes of the restaurant window. Mrs. Carter was still occupied. And still talking together was Mr. Sullivan and her grandpa who were not likely to pay a surprise visit to the newspaper office.

When she turned her bike to ride to the newspaper office, her sister Salina called out, peddling toward her. Salina came to a jerky halt. "I found Mia and told her about the meeting? But there's slight glitch. Marc and Eric have been real cow-pies today! Mom chased them out of her office after they spun themselves dizzy on her office chairs."

"After that they filled their water pistols and then caught up with me at Mia's house! They heard some of what I said to Mia. And, they want to go fishing too."

"Ugh… Those two warts! I may need to keep them close so I know where they are, but if they find out too much and blab…I'd be grounded 'til Christmas." Sonia flipped her bike's kickstand up with her foot.

"Mr. Sullivan and Grandpa are still yakking over coffee, so we know where they are. I'll get to Lost Creek as soon as I can but first I need to find Gordon, who's supposed to be with Stephen. Hanna's looking after Mrs. Carter's boys but I need to talk to her too, somehow."

Salina's mouth dropped open. "You're insane! If Mr. Sullivan found you at the newspaper that's not so bad. But Mrs. Carter could show up unexpectedly on her broomstick and – you'd be toad food!"

"I got it covered. Go on ahead with Mia, Marc and Eric. Mrs. Carter is very busy, happily making the day miserable for her staff."

Sonia hadn't told her younger sister everything but she shared more with her sister since they found the suitcase, than she had with her younger brothers.

"B-e-c-a-r-e-f-u-l. Mrs. Carter and Zara Grant's aunt are in the same bridge club. Mrs. Carter and Mrs. Knudsen might be friends."

Sonia pushed her bike to the street and just out of sight of the café window. "Those kind of people are never friends and certainly, not with each other." She rode off.

As Salina pulled her bike from behind the cast iron bench in front of the Tumbleweed Café, she spotted Philip Peters. He peddled his large tricycle toward her. His head was down, as usual. He wore his blue and red football helmet as usual and his feet were a blur, as usual.

Across the street the insurance investigator Bella Perez, had finished her interview with Sheriff Howard and his senior deputy, then the sheriff walked Ms. Perez to his patrol car. The sheriff always kept his thinning brown hair cut military short. His once muscular frame carried just a little extra weight around his midsection these days.

Sheriff Howard arranged to drive the out of state insurance investigator to Grant Ranch, and to assist with the Knudsen family interviews. As they approached the sheriff's car, the Ms. Perez noticed a little boy wearing a large football helmet peddling down the sidewalk on the other side of the main street. Pedestrians either got out
of his way or the boy weaved around them with impressive skill.

"Who's that little kid? I've seen him before. He seems to be all over this town. Where does he live?" Ms Perez looked over at Sheriff Howard.

"He lives everywhere." The sheriff grinned with his attention directed to the short, stocky object of the town's affection with big, round, hazel eyes. "Aw, that's Philip."

"Legally and officially he is Philip Peters. The mayor and his wife adopted him six years ago after he was abandoned by his mother."

"How sad." Ms. Perez was touched by the little boy she saw.

"I thought so too, at first. He seemed to have so many strikes against him. He was born with Down's syndrome, then his mother left... But the mayor and his wife stepped up and took Philip in. The mayor has two older sons at Colorado State University. Philip turned ten this past January and he's really a very bright little guy."

"You'll see him everywhere. Unofficially–he lives all over and the whole town is his family. He has his own room at the mayor's house. However, Philip might only spend two or three nights a week with the Peters. He may eat supper at Gordon McKenna's then stay the night at Mia Cho's. Or, he may eat and spend the night with Joey Salas, and his family. Philip has a very large extended circle of people who keep in close contact with the mayor and his wife and each other. That way we know where he is and who he's with."

As they talked, Philip Peters stopped his large tricycle by a bench in front of the Tumbleweed Café. By the bench was a little girl who looked to be about the same age. Her long soft brown hair was brushed back into one thick braid. Philip pulled something out of his pocket and gave it to the girl. That something was a yoyo. The little girl tried to make it spin down and then back up again. Her timing was off and she was not well coordinated.

Sheriff Howard and Ms. Perez heard the children laugh from where they stood watching from across the street. The girl handed the yoyo back to Philip, who with a practiced hand showed how the toy was suppose to work.

The sheriff shared more history. "That tricycle actually belonged to Park Sullivan our newspaper editor, when he was a boy. The things about seventy-years old."

"It is the largest tricycle I've ever seen. Usually at ten most kids are on a bicycle."

Sheriff Howard opened the passenger car door for Ms. Perez, shaking his head. "Oh no, we're not ready to give Philip that kind of mobility just yet."

****

49

Sonia spotted Stephen and Gordon leaving the newspaper office. She met them and immediately relieved them of her mother's luggage. With the grey suitcase safely in hand, she sent them to round up Joey so the team could meet at Lost Creek.

On her way home to return the grey suitcase, she spotted Hanna in the park having a picnic with Mrs. Carter's twins. Hanna waved and they met by a group of spruce trees where they could talk briefly. This was just the chance Sonia had hoped for. When Sonia finally arrived at Lost Creek, the other fishing hopefuls had already settled in at their favorite casting spots.

Naturally Philip had joined in with the group but he had to be convinced that his yoyo was not going to be effective at all in catching potential food. After Joey baited Philip's line – he walked Philip further down the creek bank some distance from the others. Philip didn't have the same mastery over casting as he had over his yoyo.

Eric was a very serious fisherman and he intended to catch more than his brother Marc. His plan was to catch enough to cook for dinner that night to impress his mom.

Mia was not interested in fishing. While all of the others actually tried to catch something, she started to read through each of the photo copies Gordon and Stephen had made. But she didn't think another meeting with Leif and Hanna missing was a good idea especially with all the other 'big-ears' close by.

Just as Sonia had arrived on her bike to join everyone, she spotted Sheriff Howard's patrol car as it crossed the bridge over Lost Creek.

The original larger group of fishing enthusiasts had drifted into two. Philip, Sonia, Gordon and Stephen had migrated toward the small, secluded area of Lost Creek where the water was deeper and almost still. Joey, Salina, Eric and Marc were on the north side of the bridge where the current ran swifter.

The section of Lost Creek that ran to the south of the bridge became a short bottleneck then spread out into a pond that was about the same shape as the wood of a golf club.

At the far edge of the pond the water flowed back out into a narrow stream where its flow picked up speed again. Lost Creek was renewed each summer by a steady mountain runoff from slow melting winter snow.

Eric was on a hot streak and caught five small trout, one right after the other. Gordon and Stephen only caught one fish apiece.

The afternoon sun was warm. Mia had dozed off with papers folded under her right hip.

Sonia sat down, by the creek bank. She held her pole just out of the water watching everyone else. She didn't know why she couldn't seem to relax and enjoy the afternoon. After all, the grey suitcase was back in her mother's closet. She had even swept off the dust and cobwebs, so new dust could settle in the attic and nothing would look disturbed. The photo copies that Gordon and Stephen made were safe with Mia.

But, she had found Hanna having a picnic with Mrs. Carters little boys and what she told Sonia played over again in her head.

Hanna overheard Mrs. Carter on the phone with someone at the ranch that Hanna was positive was Mrs. Knudsen. From Mrs. Carter's end of the phone line Hanna heard '*Oh my, of course you want this behind you. You've waited seven long years.*' This convinced Sonia even more, that seven years before, someone in the Knudsen family had committed a murder.

She wondered about the patrol car that crossed the bridge on the road to Grant Ranch. The sheriff had a passenger and Sonia was pretty sure it was the insurance lady from Des Moines. It bugged her not to know what was going on at the ranch...

Philip waded further from the shallow edge of the water. He alternated between dipping his fishing pole into the water then his bright yellow yoyo. He submerged his face just below the surface of the gentle stream.

"Philip, stop that. You'll scare the fish." Sonia shook her head.

"What fish?" Philip scowled. "I kept my eyes open but I didn't see any."

Sonia stood up and walked to the edge of the water to make sure Philip didn't wade out too far – when she spotted movement between the trees on the far banks. She shaded her eyes from the sun and saw two men fishing on the opposite side of the pond.

She couldn't make out their faces but one man appeared to be younger than the other. Both men wore long sleeved, cotton shirts and overalls. The younger man wore a baseball cap pulled down low on his forehead.

Mia opened her eyes just as Joey walked over. He held up two very tiny trout. "I only caught two. How are you guys doing?"

Philip tossed his pole onto the bank and rewound his yoyo. "Lousy."

Sonia lifted off the lid of the cooler to show Eric's spoils.

Mia stretched and stood up. "I'm no expert. I hate fish but those look very small, even to me."

Stephen retrieved his catch from the cooler and held it up. "Joey you still haven't caught any fish. What you have there is just great bait."

"I'm out of practice."

Sonia pointed to the two men fishing on the other side of the pond. "They look like they're having good luck." The two men were casting their lines again. One man looked familiar, but she could not place the second man. "Is that Mr. Tate with someone?"

Mia shrugged and shook her head.

Stephen answered. "Yup, the older guy is Silas Tate. The young guy wearing the cap must be his grandson. I think his name is Luke. Mr. Tate comes into our market now and then. You remember Mr. Tate, he raises pigs and turkeys on about fifty acres, eight miles south-west of here."

"Dad said Mr. Tate has a daughter. She moved away then showed up several years back with Luke who was oh, ten or eleven. She stayed for a couple of years then took off again, leaving Luke behind with his grandparents. They don't leave the farm much. Mrs. Tate home schooled Luke."

Gordon looked up from casting his rod again. "Man not having to go to school. That's terrific."

Stephen waved his arm and called out to Silas Tate. Mr. Tate waved back.

The young man wearing the cap, watched from across the pond as he reeled in his fishing line. He gave a shy wave then moved to a different fishing spot a short distance from Mr. Tate.

CHAPTER SEVEN
Meet The Relatives

June 15…

    Ms. Perez relaxed while Sheriff Howard drove. They crossed over a bridge that spanned a waterway the sheriff called Lost Creek. There were several kids fishing below. He waved to them then named each one. She knew she couldn't remember all the first names but their last names were very familiar

    The road the sheriff followed turned north a quarter of a mile after they crossed the bridge then paralleled the flowing creek for another three miles. With a sharp turn west again the gate to the south entrance of the historic Grant Ranch came into view.

    The drive from the town of Mosquito Creek to the ranch and its' famous guest lodge Mosquito Creek Inn, took forty minutes because Sheriff Howard had taken a slightly longer route to show Ms. Perez more of the local scenery.

    The gate opening was framed by a massive base of large river rock that supported two pillars of rough cut, pine logs. The logs towered fifteen feet high. The cross piece was another thick log set in place to complete the arch. The same stone that made the pillar base ran on for a hundred feet on either side of the road from the entrance gate to form a rock wall, three feet high.

    Sky touching spruce and pine grew between the stone wall and the pasture. The old evergreens blocked much of the view of the foothills and open grazing land that fed several thousand head of beef cattle.

"These mountains and the views are stunning. I've never been this close to The Rockies before." Ms Perez bobbed her head to see between the trees.

The sheriff slowed the speed of his patrol car. "Does that help?"

"Yes. I can see glimpses between the branches. There's hundreds of those black cows out there."

"Cattle Black Angus beef cattle." The sheriff corrected. "Most of those trees were planted sometime during the late 1930s and early 1940s. The wind gets pretty wound-up around here.

Abruptly the road ahead appeared to vanish. Sheriff Howard stopped at the crest of a wide gravel road and then watched for his visitor's reaction. At the top of the hill was a sweeping view of the long, narrow valley below to the inn, and the ranch's out buildings.

A second smaller bridge crossed another curve in Lost Creek, to reach the inn. The creek continued to meander passed two hip-roof barns on the north side of the inn. From the barns the creek curved sharply south again running directly behind the inn before it angled away from the ranch yard and west again to the mountains.

Mosquito Creek Inn was a massive building of the same river rock and pine logs as the entrance gate. And the sheriff continued as tour guide. "What you see there," he pointed. "On the far side is now the front of the inn. The wide double front doors were originally the entrance to the barn. Huge wagons could fit into the barn. Henry Grant was only eighteen and his cousin Lester Kohrs, was just nineteen when they laid claim to homestead the original 150 acres. That modest beginning grew to over 18,000 acres."

"They built the barn as their first task when they arrived in the spring of 1861. The two young bachelors slept in the hayloft. The chickens, pigs, horses and cattle were kept safe in the stalls and coops below."

"That far chimney," Sheriff Howard pointed again, "vents one of the most imposing fireplaces I have ever seen. It has two hearths. The cousins not only used the entire structure for heat but one hearth was for cooking and the second one they used to forge many of their own tools."

"According to history, Henry and Lester worked the ranch alone for oh about six or seven years. Their only help was from a few members of a nearby Blackfoot tribe. Around a dozen of the braves showed up every spring when the calves were dropped and then again each fall for the round-up, branding and cattle drive to market in Helena."

"Anyway, in the summer of 1870, Henry and Lester married sisters from one of the Blackfoot families. Then, between 1871 and 1890 Henry and his wife GreyRabbit had five children – and Lester and his wife HummingBird had seven children."

Ms. Perez was fascinated by the story of a very unusual family. Sheriff Howard's account was so much better than the listed facts in Zara Grant's file. "This valley is picture perfect, how wonderful it would be to actually live here."

Her voice was barely a whisper, but her tone was wistful. "I would be thrilled to stay at Mosquito Creek Inn myself - forever. I didn't realize there would be so many buildings. It is like a mini-village."

The Sheriff continued with what he knew of the ranch. "This has always been a working ranch. The original barn was added onto several times as the two families grew then became the main house. Later the bunkhouse was built and added on to the main house. Much of what you see now was in place by the time the United States entered the Second World War. But by then the Khors half of the family sold their interest."

"When Mr. Grant's son Jon returned from college in 1970, he applied to the State of Montana to have the Grant Ranch declared a historic sight and then convinced his father to open the Ranch up as a vacation destination spot. That change sure helped the town's economy."

"There's two acres to the south of the inn where the original vegetable garden was first tilled and to this day it still provides much of the produce the inn uses for the restaurant meals. That green house at the north-west corner of the garden was also Jon's idea. From the green house the inn can harvest fresh herbs and produce for salads even in winter."

"Sometime between his return from college and petitioning the Montana Historic Society, Jon Grant married Park Sullivan's oldest daughter, Nancy and together they worked out a way of combining all the additions the main house had undergone over 110 years, in with the smoke house and the two bunk houses. So by the time their daughter Zara was born in 1976 all the new plumbing, heating and electricity was done.

Sheriff Howard took the car out of park. "Are you ready for your meeting with the family?"

"Ready as I'll ever be. Thank you. Your additional background was helpful."

As they drove across a smaller bridge, Ms. Perez noticed the road surface that brought visitors to the parking area, changed from gravel to crushed black shale. The dark rock added to the imposing, almost haunted presence of the historic inn.

The sheriff parked under a twenty-foot high portico that connected to a long, two-sided covered porch. The porch was also attached to a series of open decks furnished with several heavy wooden chairs and outdoor tables.

The tall wide, double French doors to the lobby of the inn had replaced the original barn doors. And everything Ms. Perez saw was very large and very old and very weathered, and looked as solid as all those very large, very old, very weathered mountains.

When the sheriff opened the door for Ms. Perez to step inside, the brief description of the stone fireplace didn't prepare her for what she saw in person. A twenty-six foot tower of river rock – most about the size of a cantaloupe – seemed to grow right up through the middle of a spacious forty by fifty foot room. The fireplace was a three-tiered, triangle shape that narrowed toward the roof.

As they walked around the fireplace, Sheriff Howard pointed out the smaller opening where Henry Grant and Lester Khors did their own blacksmith work and the larger opening they used for heat and to cook.

At the opposite end of the converted lobby Ms. Perez saw where the hayloft had once been. It was still an open loft area above the check-in desk, but it was now for guests to relax. Bookshelves lined the long wall and leather chairs were scattered about this space to sit.

A strong perfume caused Ms. Perez to blink. She turned to see Zigvarta Knudsen face to face. Ms. Perez recognized the older woman from the photo in Zara Grant's file. Though the guardian of Grant Ranch was now seventy-three, she had not changed much from the newspaper picture of her at the age of sixty-six when Zara went missing. Mrs. Knudsen still wore her hair up in two rows of long braids wrapped around the crown of her head. And she still didn't smile.

"I will dispense with many of the social tasks required of me when I greet a guest at the inn, Ms. Perez." She nodded to the sheriff, "Mr. Howard." Then she addressed the insurance investigator again.

"I can appreciate that you are away from home and would like to return just as quickly as my family and I would like to put the last seven years completely behind us. My reception office is this way. "

Ms. Perez looked at Sheriff Howard, who shrugged as they followed the stately slightly overweight woman. The investigator realized that Mrs. Knudsen was impatient to have the insurance company declare her great-niece Zara Grant, legally dead.

Mrs. Knudsen led the officer and the investigator passed the check-in desk then down a short hallway to a small corner room. Even though the room was located on the north side of the inn it was bright with natural light from a wall of floor to ceiling windows. Four large, green leather chairs set in front of a chrome and black, cast iron stove, was the room's only seating. On a round oak table placed in the center of the circle of chairs was a large glass coffee pot, three cups and a plate of tempting cookies.

"My mother Greta was born in Norway as was my great uncle Lester Kohrs. Since I took over running the inn, all of the breads, desserts and much of the meals for which we are now famous, are Norwegian. You may sit. I can offer you coffee?"

The coffee smelled strong. Sheriff Howard shook his head. Ms. Perez nodded. "Yes please."

The investigator opened her briefcase. She retrieved a pen along with a tabbed, three ring binder and flipped to the label marked; *Interviews.*

Mrs. Knudsen didn't pour a coffee for herself. She chose to sit in a chair across from the sheriff. Her back was ruler straight. She was not relaxed but perched at the edge of the seat cushion, clearly considering the people in the room with her as intruders.

Ms. Perez began. "Mrs. Knudsen, in my letter I had requested the opportunity to meet with all of your family members. Are your two sons and their wives available to join us now or will I need to return another day?"

"I received your letter. A copy was sent to the ranch attorney, who did not see the need of an interview with either of my sons or their wives. They were in Minnesota when Zara disappeared. In fact they did not come to Montana until after my brother – their uncle Khors, died."

"Mrs. Knudsen, my company's normal procedure is to automatically close a file and certify our declaration seven years and one day after the documented date of a recorded disappearance."

"However, six months ago a certified letter arrived at our office. It was addressed to my former manager who was the original insurance investigator when Zara was reported missing. The letter was postmarked Helena. There was no return address on the letter or envelop. The letter was unsigned. The paper was common white stock, sold for any standard, computer printer."

"The author of the letter made some disturbing statements and posed some very interesting questions. Because the letter was unsigned, I was not prepared to rush to judgment or come to any quick conclusions when it was forwarded to me. I was however, obligated to do what I could to look further. Therefore…I need to interview you Mrs. Knudsen, both of your sons and both of their wives."

****

Sonia's curiosity grew steadily as the minutes ticked away to a full hour. She had trouble pretending to fish after seeing the sheriff's car cross the bridge toward the ranch.

Mia and the other members of the sleuthing team were curious too. Curious and anxious. An afternoon fishing had not turned out to be the great cover idea for a second meeting as originally thought. There were too many other snoopy little eyes and ears, attached to big mouths.

The new detectives, who badly wanted to know what the insurance lady was doing at the inn, finally couldn't stand it any longer. But Mia and Joey had to go home soon so that left just Sonia, Stephen and Gordon.

Sonia couldn't take the chance that Marc and Eric would want to follow so leaving Salina to watch them and Philip too, Sonia made up a flimsy excuse about a new scavenger hunt. Then they quickly took off on their bikes.

They cycled straight north for a full mile out of sight of the fishing party, then they walked their bikes across a second narrow bend in Lost Creek to the ranch.

Continuing to push their bikes from the road through a narrow band of wild flowers and buffalo grass, Stephen suddenly began to panic. "Hold it a minute."

Gordon and Sonia who were slightly ahead stopped walking their bikes.

"What's our plan?"

Gordon looked to Sonia.

Sonia had no plan.

"I mean, do we try to sneak in unseen or do we continue with our ever expanding list of lies and make up a reason to be there?"

Sonia had a flash of inspiration. "Anna! Anna might be home"

Gordon rolled his eyes. "You better hope she's not. You two haven't liked each other since she moved here in the first grade. If you suddenly showed up asking for her that would look weird."

"Gordon and I better go on our own."

"What's *your* story going to be then?"

Stephen smiled. "I have a great one and it won't even be a lie. Archery lessons! Anna's always been impressed by the Olympic medals my dad won for Norway. When Anna found out that Leif and I learned to shoot, she wanted to try too."

"That's a brilliant idea." Gordon looked a Sonia. "Even if Anna isn't at home, since she's going into grade seven with us, none of her family will think it unusual that we stopped by."

Sonia blushed, dark, pink. She was furious but knew they were right. "Okay. If, Anna's not home you're off the hook but if she's there – where's your bow?

Stephen hesitated for barely a second. "Bitter Root Crossing. Leif and I have a target and two of dad's old bows stashed there. If Anna's home, it's just two miles due south of here."

"Fine." Sonia squared her shoulders and turned her bike back toward the fishing pond. "I better rescue my sister, and make sure that none of the others have drowned or drowned each other."

CHAPTER EIGHT
Connecting Some Dots

June 17…

As a cover for another detective meeting, Sonia, Hanna and Mia started a Scrabble game. Copies of all meager evidence were safely tucked under the dining room table at their feet inside Mia's pink backpack that was a portable office of sorts.

Sonia's Aunt Monica was on temporary leave from her job at the bank. She slept late every morning then hung around the house watching movies with Marc and Eric. This saved Sonia a lot of babysitting time but everyone hanging around interfered with her mystery solving time.

The friends had the house to themselves only because by noon, Sonia was actually able to talk her aunt into taking the boys out for a hotdog lunch at Wally's.

Sonia and Mia didn't share the same doubts that Stephen did. They were convinced that Zara Grant's disappearance and the death of Khors Grant were both connected. And the cause of both was - murder. Sonia had written the details of their suspicions in her diary the night before. So there it was, permanently in ink.

Most of the copied information from the grey suitcase had been disappointing. The news accounts published in the *Review* were not very detailed, which made sense. The disappearance was a local story and in a small town everyone already knew almost everything. And none of the other Montana papers of August or September 1990 printed much about the teenagers' disappearance after their initial front page story.

What had convinced Sonia and Mia of the double plot appeared in two nationally published sources. The first story was published in *Time* magazine January 1991, three months after Kohrs Grant had died. Then, a second article in February 1991 that was in *Forbes* magazine - sealed their theory.

The entire history of the Grant family had been published in *Time*. When *Forbes* published the financial details from cattle ranching to coal mining, to the discovery of oil and natural gas, the motive was even greater than Mia and Sonia imagined. Not even Sonia's Aunt Monica had any idea how wealthy her best friend would have been.

Sonia and Mia could hardly wait to show the magazine stories to Stephen. "Not just money was the motive, but h-u-g-e money was the motive." Sonia played with the letter tiles on her tray. "Hanna, what did your Mom say about her work at the inn?"

Hanna Gaikis laughed. "Well, Mom doesn't know I read those old articles so she now thinks I must have this amazing memory, cause I was only five when she was fired. Anyway, when she managed the inn restaurant, she was also in charge of the green house, the garden and the entire menu."

"My mother was accused of stealing food. Two other staff said they saw my mom load food into her car from the pantry and the green house on two occasions. Both of the so-called witnesses were here from Poland on expired visas. But Mom said that she knew it was all a trumped up reason when Mrs. Knudsen, gave her an envelope with $2,000 cash and a letter of recommendation."

Mia was furiously taking notes as Hanna talked.

"My mom's friend Louise was Manager of Reservations and Assistant Manager of the inn. She was fired the same day as my mom for flirting with the guests."

"Some very famous people vacation at the inn to get away to a quiet place. And according to my mom, Louise joked about finding herself a rich husband from among the guests at the inn, but she didn't do anything. Mom thought Mrs. Knudsen wasn't justified in dismissing her friend either. Both friends were fired on the same day and the reason was a complete lie."

"Hanna, your mother probably knows something." Mia Cho owned a paperback copy of every mystery Agatha Christie had ever wrote. "But she doesn't *know* what she knows. That often happens in these situations."

Sonia tried to make sense of where they were going. "Okay, what do *we* know? My head is filled with 'stuff' I'm trying to sort. We have a suitcase of news clippings and Zara's diary where she wrote that her Aunt Zigvarta was nice to her only when there were other people around. So we have a missing girl and her grandfather who had a heart attack...."

Mia jumped in. "I read that a heart attack can be brought on by several poisons that can't be detected by an autopsy.

Hanna was amazed. "Really?"

Then Sonia held up her fingers, counting. "We have Zara Grant and Kohrs Grant both out of the way of a giant pile of money. We have Zigvarta Knudsen who does not even pretend to be nice after her brother dies. We have her snooty sons who might as well have a ring through their noses because their mother leads them around like they've had their brains sucked out of their heads."

Hanna interjected. "Oh, and don't forget delightful Anna Knudsen. Did you now she has actually hinted that her family is related to Norwegian and Polish royalty? Anna's mother and aunt had lunch one time at the Tumbleweed and didn't leave my mom a tip. Royalty? I'd really like the chance to tell off *her royal hinny.*"

Sonia dropped her hand into her lap. "All we have is a lot of motive. But we have no means and no opportunity. But worse than that we're the only ones who think there was actually a crime. We need a crime."

Mia was excited. "So let's make our next move Zara's grandfather. Let's look for poisons that can cause heart attacks? Maybe Zara was poisoned too"

"Poison is the most common form of murder method for women." Mia had stacked her letter tiles up like poker chips. "Some of those plants still grow wild in the forest or jungles."

"Wait a minute." Sonia began to pick up the tiles from the center of the Scrabble board and put them away. "What about the green house? Zigvarta the witch could be growing poisonous herbs. Mia could be right Hanna, your mom was in charge of the green house. She may have seen a new plant but didn't think of it as important."

Hanna handed her tiles to Sonia. "Mushrooms." Was all she said.

"That's it." Mia agreed. "We need to check out that green house."

"My Mother and Louise Garcia were fired almost seven years ago." Hanna said. "I really don't think any of the Knudsen's are that stupid."

Sonia finished collecting all of the tiles and put them into the old draw-string bag her mother had made to hold the jacks she got for her sixth birthday. "No they aren't that stupid but they are that arrogant – and that sometimes makes people sloppy. We need to go out to the ranch."

"Count me out." Hanna leaned forward. "Didn't Stephen and Gordon go out there the day before yesterday?"

Sonia nodded. "Anna wasn't home. Apparently her *royalness* was shopping with her mom in Great Falls. Gordon and Stephen only got as far as the lobby and the front breakfast room. They bought a soda and hung out on one of the decks. From a gardener they found out that one by one Mrs. Knudsen, both of her sons and one of the wives were called into Mrs. Knudsen's office and then questioned separately by Sheriff Howard and that insurance lady."

"By the time they got to the other side of the inn and found the right window for Mrs. Knudsen's office, there were two ranch hands in the corral directly across the road, practicing their roping."

Mia stuffed her notebook into her backpack. "Let's actually make up another scavenger hunt game, with a list of stuff we need to find. That will give us a good excuse if we get caught snooping."

Sonia closed the lid on the Scrabble box. "Of course then know one will suspect anything. Tomorrow morning we can meet at the market and head out on our bikes. I'll ask my Aunt Monica will watch Marc, Eric and Salina."

Hanna shook her head. "Sorry I don't have an aunt I must baby-sit Mrs. Carter's boys again tomorrow. I only got off today because Mrs. Carter's mother was visiting from Butte.

"I am so game!" Mia grinned. "But if we're right, we shouldn't be going out to the ranch alone. Maybe Joey can go with us. His grandparents don't open the restaurant until noon. And maybe Gordon could come too. He's only helping his grandfather at the newspaper two days a week."

"I know." Sonia was tempted to include the boys especially Gordon but her mother had lectured her extensively against romance – particularly when the love-struck was only in grade six. Sonia did not want to relive that conversation again anytime soon.

Sonia asked Mia to phone Joey Salas and Gordon McKenna. "With Monica here almost all of the time and my brothers' loose-lips, the atmosphere around here is a little, tense. I might not get a chance to use the phone privately. There's one in the kitchen and an extension in my mom's bedroom. But I couldn't even risk using the one in my mom's office."

Mia nodded, thinking she understood. "Sure I'll call."

****

The following morning Grandpa was seated at the kitchen table feeding toast chunks to Joker while reading that morning's edition, of *USA Today*. Sonia poured her orange juice and waited for her toast to pop up. Joker came over and licked her hand. Grandpa had run out of toast but Joker smelled more coming.

As she looked down at the splotched patterns on the friendly, fury face she decided to take Joker along to the ranch. Protection he was not but none of the Knudsen's knew that Joker was about as threatening as pudding.

"Good grief." Grandpa spoke up. "I didn't realize that it's been that long."

Sonia ignored Jokers big brown eyes. He wasn't supposed to have any toast. She sat down in a chair across from the back of the opened newspaper. "What happened long ago?"

Grandpa turned the page. His voice still came from behind the newsprint. "Oh that little baby girl who got stuck in a well in Tennessee, she's in school now."

"She got stuck in a well?"

"Yup. Took them two days to get her out. Real heart-stopping drama. I'm surprised we haven't had some kid get stuck in a well here." He put down the newspaper.

"There are old water wells in the back yards of nearly all the houses in Mosquito Creek that were built before 1960 and hundreds of mining company core wells in the foot hills."

He went back to turning the pages of his newspaper. "All very dangerous for young kids."

Sonia stopped chewing her toast in mid bite. She had a horrible, but revealing thought then shivered as the possibilities settled in.

CHAPTER NINE
Another Scavenger Hunt

June 18...

Sonia had arranged to meet Mia behind Anderlund's Market at the south end of town. She took Joker just in case either Gordon or Joey couldn't make it. But as she waited for the traffic to pass so she could cross the highway, Sonia spotted Mia waiting with both Gordon and Joey. Joker recognized them too and barked.

"I finished the briefing." Mia greeted Sonia as if she worked for the FBI.

Sonia handed out the list of items for their scavenger hunt - trespassing excuse. "Let's make it girls against the guys – if anyone should ask. Joker is for protection."

Joker heard his name and wagged his tail.

The kids took off on their bikes using the shortcut across country. It was a clear sunny day with just a slight breeze. Joker darted about sniffing the air and the ground.

By cycling across country and avoiding the roads – the foursome reached the crest of the steep road that overlooked Mosquito Creek Inn and all its out buildings in twenty-seven minutes. Joker ran on down the hill took a drink at the creek then loped back.

Gordon turned to the others. "I think that we should follow the same rules that we did for the two real scavenger hunts we had last summer. Joey and I will head down first." He looked from Mia to Sonia.

"You two show up about eight minutes from now as if you're running a little behind and we're winning. How does that sound?"

"Like fiction." Mia giggled. "We won both times last summer."

Joey shook his head.

The boys peddled down the steep gravel road at a slight angle then crossed over to the grassy hill until they reached the level bottom. They cycled over the bridge and disappeared behind the long narrow hen house. Joker nuzzled Sonia then laid down by her in the grass.

"Gordon and Joey are heading for the opposite side of the inn." Mia turned to Sonia. "That was a good strategy. Now we can start with the greenhouse."

"That's fine but we still don't know what we are looking for."

Mia checked her watch. "We don't need to." She held up a clear plastic bag. "We can collect one leaf from every plant we find in the greenhouse then show them to Mr. Hawkins. He'll be able to tell us."

Mr.Hawkins was the high school science teacher. Because LaBarge High was a small school, Mr. Hawkins taught physics, chemistry and biology. When he moved to Mosquito Creek to teach, he bought the house next door to the Cho family.

Mia checked the time again. "Another two minutes. I think Gordon likes you."

Sonia could feel her face color change. "Really? Why do you think that?"

"Because he's always looking at you to see if you're looking at him."

"My brother Eric ran off at the mouth about me liking Gordon to my mother. The timing could not have been worse. Eric is such a snot-ball sometimes. My mother had a serious melt-down. She has outlawed any form of dating until I'm fourteen!"

"Yikes." Mia was supportive but could not entirely identify with Sonia's crisis.

"I might as well live in a convent!"

Joker listened to the rise and fall of voices.

"I don't know if the Catholic Church has convents anymore."

Sonia sighed. "Then I'm even worse off than I thought."

Mia caught sight of Joey and Gordon off in the distance. They pushed their bikes toward the horse barn on the east side of the corral. She checked her watch. "Okay, now we can go."

Both girls chose to walk their bikes part of the way down the side of the steep road. Just before the bottom, Mia hopped on coasting across the bridge with her feet up on her handle bars. Sonia was right behind her with Joker back on the leash.

From the gravel driveway they took a brick walkway on the north boundary of the vegetable garden. After leaning their bikes into the branches of a thick spruce, they made straight for the greenhouse. They expected the door to be open and it was. Sonia hooked Joker's leash to a water tap.

Inside the greenhouse, Mia pulled out her scavenger hunt list. "Let's start over there and come back to the door in a big loop."

Sonia nodded. She was nervous even with the scavenger hunt story. As the girls walked between the raised beds of plants, they snapped off one leaf from any plant they couldn't identify. An overhead fan cycled on that also sent out a puff of mist. The sudden noise with the vapor startled both girls. When the fan abruptly shut off again, the green house was eerily silent.

"I do not remember inviting either of you to my home." Anna Knudsen appeared from nowhere. The high-pitched tone of her voice was brittle ice. She was a younger, slimmer version of her paternal grandmother.

Spunky Mia recovered her wits first. "This is not your home. And, neither is the inn for that matter. You live in a hotel for heaven's sake."

"This ranch is my entire home, thank you. And that *hotel* as you call it is for invited guests only. You're trespassing."

Sonia's heart slowed enough for her to speak. "Anna, there is a large tour bus pulling up outside. This is a historic sight. We're not hurting anything."

"Well unless you can show me your ticket for the guided-tour you need to leave. What's that piece of paper?"

Mia had forgotten it was in her hand. "We're on a scavenger hunt." For a split second Mia thought Anna actually looked disappointed that she was not included. Then Mia had a flash of inspiration. "Would you like to join us? Gordon and Joey are well ahead of us. We could use some help."

"Gordon is here too, where?"

Shaken by this surprising turn of events, Sonia didn't know which one she wanted to shake first, Mia or Anna. She hadn't considered that she might have competition for Gordon. Her heart sank as she forgot the task at hand.

Anna was Gordon's age. They both would be at the junior high school in the fall. Anna had a clear field for at least the next year. Longer - if Sonia's mother didn't relent about when she could date. Sonia felt like committing murder herself – and she thought she might start with her big-mouth-brother…Eric.

Fortunately Mia was still on target. "I don't know where Gordon and Joey are. They've been ahead of us the entire morning. They may have left by now to go on to the next item on our list." Mia grabbed Sonia's hand. "We better go, bye."

They squeezed between Anna and a section of budding mushrooms under darkened glass. Back outside, Sonia grabbed Joker's leash. They ran for their bikes and peddled back to the bridge checking over their shoulder as if they were being chased by flying vampires.

They stopped at the base of the hill and looked back. The greenhouse looked empty. No Anna in sight. There was no sign of Joey or Gordon either. Joker wagged his tail then sat waiting for the next adventure.

Mia laid her bike down then sat in the grass at the edge of the gravel road. "I don't think I'll make a good detective after all. I almost wet my pants back there and it was only Anna who found us."

Sonia was even more determined than ever to prove Anna's family had committed a crime. "I had no idea she liked Gordon. She has lots of money, she's smart and she's older…"

Mia interrupted. "A has a grandmother who's not going to let Anna date Gordon McKenna! To Zigvarta Knudsen, we're all something unmentionable that you throw away in a tissue. Besides which you ninny, Anna and Gordon are second cousins or something. Have you forgotten? Gordon's mom and Zara Grant's mom were sisters.
Mr. Grant was Mrs. Knudsen brother."

Sonia had forgotten and Mia's reminder changed her mood. But she still wanted to prove the entire family including Anna, were just plain criminals.

They spotted the boys riding across the bridge. Gasping for air they reached the girls and joined them in a heap of legs and arms on the ground.

"We were chased out of the garage." Gordon panted. "Anna's dad was not amused or sympathetic to two kids struggling with a scavenger hunt list."

"We snuck in with the tour of the horse barn and the hen house but got busted when we left the group for the machine shed. It's attached to the back of the garage. Man! The ranch has every kind of mechanical gadget you can imagine."

Joey grinned. "Besides having every mechanical gadget, they can repair any kind of engine, even the huge generator that pumps water from the two wells used by the inn and the other buildings. But all that equipment could make burying someone very deep – very easy."

Sonia came alive. "Wells! That was another idea I wanted to check out. My grandpa was talking about some little kid who got stuck in a well. He said there are dozens of abandoned coal and water wells around here. But we'll need to find out where they are and then invent a story that explains why we want to look for them."

"Finding the well locations is easy." Gordon smiled at Sonia. "Remember, my dad's a forest ranger and my grandfather has multiple copies of forestry maps at the newspaper office."

Joey looked puzzled. "Wait a minute. I thought we were looking for evidence of a poisoning?"

"We are." Mia confirmed.

"Actually, Mia and I think Zara was made to disappear and her grandfather was poisoned. So, we're looking for proof of two murders but two different methods."

Sonia explained. "Zara Grant actually vanished but no one found her body. Mr. Grant, who had been healthy, died suddenly two months later in October."

Mia was excited again. She felt like Agatha Christie herself. "A truly cleaver murderer changes their MO, so they're not a suspect."

Sonia stood up looking at Gordon. "Do you think your dad or your grandfather would let us have a copy of maps that show both town water wells and the mining core wells?"

"Sure but what do we tell them? They'll ask why we're suddenly so interested in abandoned wells?"

Everyone else stood up too. Joker got up again as well and stretched. They all picked up their bikes to walk them back up the hill.

"We could use the newspaper article my grandpa told me about." Sonia offered. "Maybe your grandfather would even write a feature on the wells around here."

Gordon was impressed. "Nice. You're very good at this investigative stuff."

"Yeah but I don't like the part where someone like Douglas Knudsen grabs a guy by the arm and shoves him out the door." Joey had almost wet his pants too.

CHAPTER TEN
Unusual Discovery

June 19…

Gordon was returning to his grandfather's newspaper office when he spotted the insurance lady. Ms. Perez had parked in front of the sheriff's office and was running up the front steps. She looked like she was in a hurry about something.

He checked his watch and figured he could spare another ten minutes, or so. He had finished his task of refilling each one of the newspaper dispensing boxes around town, so there was really nothing pressing on his time at that moment.

Since the wagon he used to take papers from box to box was still attached to his bike, he decided to leave his bike parked next to Hartley's Photo Studio and walk across the street.

As he approached the front doors of the sheriff's office, he began to panic when he reached the second step. If someone asks me, he wondered…'Why am I here?'

The doors opened and Mrs. Spear, Sheriff Howard's office manager, came down the steps toward him carrying mail for the post office. "Hi Gordon did you lose something?"

There it was Gordon's reason why. "Hi Mrs. Spear. Yeah, I need to check the board. I lost a very nice kite a few days ago."

They passed each other and when Gordon had reached the top step Mrs. Spear had reached the sidewalk. "Well, good luck." She waved then walked toward the post office.

He hurried inside heading straight for the bulletin board the sheriff put up for community posters and lost and found notices. As he stood staring at random pieces of paper, he felt guilty. He was sure that somewhere between *Heaven* and *Hell* there was a place called *Detention* for kids who lied. Gordon wasn't sure he could be a detective if lying was one of the job skills.

The door to the sheriff's office was open but he was not at his desk. Gordon heard muffled voices that came from behind the closed door to the conference room. He moved to the far end of the bulletin board trying to hear actual words.

The phone rang on Mrs. Spear's desk and Gordon jumped. The conference room door opened and the sheriff took three swift strides to answer it. He gave Gordon a smile and a half nod. "Mosquito Creek Sheriff's office, Sheriff Howard speaking."

Gordon felt his cheeks go hot. He kept his face toward the bulletin board, hoping no one would notice, while his heart tried to punch its way out of his chest.

"That's great." The sheriff responded from his end of the phone line. "Just fax it over anytime. Thanks." He replaced the receiver. "Hi there Gord, whad'ya loose?"

"Aw, my kite sir." Gordon felt sick. That was it, he thought. I'm going right passed *Detention* and straight to *Hell*. Now I've lied to a police officer.

"Good luck. There's lot of paper tacked up there." The sheriff returned to the conference room but didn't close the door completely.

Gordon regained his nerve and changed his mind about leaving. With the door left partially open he could hear the rustle of paper and every word that was said.

"It's a good thing we recorded each of the interviews,' said Sheriff Howard, "as well as taking notes. How far apart is everyone's story?"

There was the sound of more paper, then the voice of Ms. Perez. "Far enough to park a Grant Ranch tour bus in the space. I worked all night on these transcripts. I made three copies at the library earlier this morning. There's one for me, for you and your senior deputy to read."

The sheriff spoke. "You'd think they had enough time to put together the same script by now."

"Actually time has worked to our advantage." Ms. Perez explained. "Seven years ago they would have been on guard and somewhat prepared for this type of questioning. But they weren't expecting any further investigation. So when I arrived - remembering what they needed to forget - became more difficult."

"I'm sure any good lawyer could argue that all we have is some conflicting, memories from the passage of a lot of time," responded Sheriff Howard.

"I think it's enough," argued Ms. Perez. "Added to the information from the people I found in Minnesota too, I have good reason to search further."

Sheriff Howard spoke again. "Well you can bet the Knudsen's are comparing notes now and the next time we go back their memories will be very clear and their stories will match perfectly."

The investigator lowered her voice. "If that happens, it will make their situation look worse. I do have the authority to delay the final declaration if I have discovered enough evidence to cast doubt about Zara Grant's disappearance. If I can show even some reasonable evidence for a suspicion of foul play, the estate can remain in limbo until a Montana judge reviews all of the new findings."

"We know from the two people I interviewed in Minnesota, that both brothers came to Montana three times before Zara disappeared." More paper shifted. "And, Douglas flew to Montana at least once between Zara's disappearance and Grant Kohrs' death. I have travel agency records and copies of tickets from airline microfiche files. But all of the flights are either to Billings or Great Falls. I haven't been able to find evidence of a car rental or any other means of transportation that physically puts one or both of the Knudsen brothers in Mosquito Creek."

Gordon could hardly believe what he was hearing. Stephen might be totally wrong and Sonia might be completely right. A normal week for the Mosquito Creek sheriff and his staff was looking for lost wallets, writing speeding tickets, sorting out minor fender dents and bar arguments. This - could be national news!

"Besides my senior deputy Ms. Perez, I have two other officers. Tell me how you would like to proceed and I'll find the people to help you however, they would be officers borrowed from other communities."

There was the sound of a closing briefcase. "I understand Sheriff."

The tone from the insurance investigator was kinda snooty, Gordon thought.

"I'll drive to Great Falls then to Billings myself to see what I can discover from there. While I am gone, I would appreciate some help in hiding the fact that I am away."

"Everyone knows my car. I would like to leave it here and the keys with you. If your deputies could move it from time to time, that would be a great help. I'll rent a car in Helena. I should be back in three days provided I don't accidentally end up lost somewhere in Alberta because I took a wrong turn, somewhere in this huge state. I dread getting into a car to drive more miles. From Iowa to Montana was a lot of highway! But it can't be helped. I believe I'm onto something. Zara Grant may very well have disappeared at the hands of one or more members of the Knudsen family."

Gordon heard the sound of moving chairs. He started to move toward the door to the front of the office then he spotted Mrs. Spear coming back up the steps. Looking for a lost kite was one thing, but he was pretty sure he'd be grounded for the rest of his natural life if Sheriff Howard discovered Gordon had stayed to listen to a conversation that was really not for his ears.

Hunched down, Gordon hurried toward the office furniture on the opposite side of the room. He had just enough time to hide behind the desk of one of the deputies.

Sheriff Howard's voice grew louder as the meeting broke up and the adults walked to the outer office. "We'll move your car for you. Guess you'll need a ride to Helena."

"That would be appreciated. I'd like to leave sometime just after dark."

From his hiding place under the spare desk, Gordon heard the door open and Mrs. Spear's clogs thumped across the wooden floor. "It's warm out there. And look at all this mail. Most of its just junk. Are you leaving Ms. Perez?"

The front door opened again. "Yes Mrs. Spear, I'm finished here for now." Then the door closed.

"Sheriff, will you listen for the phone? I needed to visit the ladies room?"

"Sure."

"I can get the phone from my office." Sheriff Howard sounded weary. "I need to look at a possible change in the patrol schedule."

Gordon heard their feet walk away. Next he heard water running from behind the *Ladies-Room* door. He peaked out and around the corner of the desk. With his heart kicking at his ribs again he crouched low, and tiptoed quickly out the side door, that lead to the alley.

CHAPTER ELEVEN
Everyone Loves A Parade

June 21…

"I have another super-brilliant idea for a float entry in the parade." Leif waved a roll of paper in the air at his older brother. "We'll be in the prize money for sure."

Stephen was perched on a ladder to replace three light bulbs over the closed bins of dried herbs. "Not another one!" He climbed down the ladder. "We'da gotta prize all right with your first idea!"

Leif followed his brother to the front of the store, defending his position. "Everyone knows Penny and Nickel. The cage would've been easy to make out'a clothes hangers. The tourists would've remembered the store. It would've been an advertising imprint."

"*Advertising imprint?* Where do you get this stuff? Anyway, it wasn't the tourists I was worried about." Stephen handed Leif a broom pointing to the floor under the bird cage. "You and me dressed as two oversized blue and green parakeets, inside a clothes-hanger cage would have made an *imprint* all right and us, the punch line to every joke in town for–the–rest–of–our–lives!"

Leif, took the broom and handed Stephen the role of paper. "Well you'll like this one." He began to sweep the feathers, seeds and litter from under the cage.

Stephen had just unrolled his brother's drawing when their younger stepsister, Heather came rushing up to the front of the store.

"I'm desperate," Heather pleaded. "Is there something very important that you need me to help you with? Anything!"

Leif stopped sweeping. Stephen looked puzzled.

"Mother is obsessed with her booth. We have hundreds of those silk flowers and dozens of those goofy pots. I'm starting to have nightmares!"

Leif shook his head and continued to sweep his small pile right out of the store's front door. Stephen shrugged.

"Ugh! I'm doomed." Heather sighed then trudged back to the rear of the store.

Stephen and Leif decided the fuss over some dumb flowers arranged in even dumber red, clay pots, was a whole lot of drama they preferred to avoid.

Their life with their dad before he remarried had been simple and peaceful without tears or hysterics. They had no memory of their mother. She died from complications of pneumonia when Stephen was four years-old and Leif was three.

While Heather's mom and their dad dated, nothing during those months seemed to affect the boys directly. But after the wedding, two females suddenly in their house everyday - all day - was like a fast splash of cold water shot from a garden hose.

To avoid as much of the growing, daily chaos as possible the boys volunteered for more tasks and responsibility at their dad's market.

Normally the brothers looked forward to the annual rodeo. But this year, they wanted to leave town for somewhere else…anywhere else. They felt sorry for their dad and for their stepsister Heather. There was no escape for either of them.

To kick-off the Rodeo Mosquito Creek held an opening day parade. The Chamber of Commerce expected all of the local business owners to enter a float or participate in the parade with some type of display on wheels, or on foot.

Their dad had been distracted earlier in the spring with his wedding plans and then he became just as caught up with helping his new wife build and stock her booth at the fairgrounds.

So that the market would have an entry, Stephen originally planned to decorate his bike with large painted cutouts of produce attached to the fenders and handle bars. Leif had much grander ideas. Neither boy was old enough to drive so Leif had revised his original idea with a float that could fit on a small flat-bed garden wagon they could hitch to their dad's riding lawn mower. Leif wanted the float to standout from the other local business entries.

First prize, for the most creative float was a $500 gift certificate from Trask Hardware & Sporting Goods, offered by Mayor Peters. The boys had a lot of plans for the camping equipment they could buy there, if they won that.

Second prize was a $300 gift certificate to Les Tres Luna Restaurant, offered by Joey's grandparents Rosa and Ricardo Salas. The boys liked the idea of several dinners out, for the best Mexican food on-the-planet.

Third prize was a $150 gift certificate to the Hansen's Theater, offered by Lee Cho who had acquired half interest in the town's sole movie theater when one of his clients, could not pay all of his accounting bill. Going to several movies for free was also appealing to the boys.

With the chance for one of the three prizes as their incentive, Leif got Stephen onboard for his alternative idea and they set to work to enter a float they were sure would be a winner.

****

Gordon McKenna was back at the newspaper and sat with his youngest sister Alyson, on a stack of newly printed rodeo posters. Despite the heat he tried to keep the melting strawberry ice cream from dripping off the cone onto his lap.

Philip sat on the floor beside the same stack of posters. His chocolate cone was disappearing so quickly that dripping was not Philip's problem, but getting it in his mouth without smearing ice cream from one ear to the other, kinda was.

For most of the morning, the two younger kids had helped Gordon, his mom and his grandfather Mr. Sullivan, with the rodeo posters and other advertising. After they were printed, the younger kids had bundled and tied the advertising posters to put up on storefronts, bulletin boards and sign posts all over Mosquito Creek and Powell County and then to other businesses in the larger neighboring cities of Butte and Helena.

Gordon's mother backed the newspaper's cargo van to the rear loading dock. When she came around to the loading dock, Philip jumped up stuffing the last of his cone into his mouth. Chocolate oozed from the corners of his lips and down his chin. His cheeks were so full of ice cream and cone he could hardly chew.

"Who gave you ice cream?"

Philip lifted up his t-shirt to wipe his face. "Your dad." He grinned.

"Grandfather said it was our lunch break." Alyson explained to her mother.

Mrs. McKenna rolled her eyes. "Okay you two back inside. It's a good thing the bundles of posters and newspapers are wrapped in thick brown paper." Even with the remains of Philip's chocolate cone ground into the front of his shirt, his face and hands were grim. "Gordon, are you almost done?"

"I can finish it." Philip made a grab for Gordon's strawberry cone.

"No way." Gordon changed hands and jumped down from the stack of posters. He disappeared through the double swinging doors to the front office area of the weekly newspaper.

"I guess that just leaves you and me pal." Mrs. McKenna opened the back door to the van then spread out a plastic tarp inside across the metal floor. "Just take one bundle at a time Philip. Any more is too heavy. Okay?"

"O-kay."

They loaded four bundles of posters destined for Helena and Butte, into the van first. Gordon and Mr. Sullivan returned through the double swings doors. Gordon carried two roles of masking tape and his grandfather carried a staple gun with two boxes of staples. Together they finished loading the van with the posters and newspapers, ready to distribute. Gordon picked up the small strands of twine and end pieces of the brown wrapping paper. "Mom, can we get some lunch before we go?"

"Didn't you get an ice cream cone?" His mother asked.

"Yeah, we did. We got an ice cream cone and gummy bears."

"Dad! What have you been feeding the children?"

"Oh the usual food groups." Mr. Sullivan winked at his daughter. "A little dairy and a lot of sugar."

"You're supposed to be a role model." She gave her dad a hug then pulled away. "How come you never gave me ice cream and gummy bears when I worked here as a kid?"

"Because your mother worked here too, remember?"

"Oh yeah. Do you want to grab a quick hot dog with us. I gotta give those kids something decent for lunch."

"Right. French fries and hot dogs. There's another food group!"

"If that's a no, then we're off. I'm taking Philip too. Please call his mother. We could be late, maybe seven o'clock."

****

"They're tipping 'cause you're leaving too much stem." Mia coached her younger sister.

This year it was Niki's job to cut the carnations just below the blooms then float them in the aluminum water trough to keep them fresh. But several of the blooms had tipped over and floated on their side. "This is so b-o-r-i-n-g. Trade ya?'

"Okay but you can't hurry. Mom likes the cut ribbon measured exactly three feet, four feet and five feet." Mia held a pair of florist's shears in one hand and a new role of purple ribbon in the other. She had already cut multiple lengths of ribbon from large rolls of various widths, patterns and colors.

Niki hesitated. "Nah, I'll cut stems."

Between cutting ribbon and stems, the girls also looked after customers who walked in to place orders or to buy potted plants and ready made arrangements for sale.

Their mother and aunt had been up and at the store by six that morning to receive a truck load of fresh flowers and greenery. With numerous local weddings in June and an increase in the number of businesses entering floats for the parade this year - the *Petals Flower Shoppe* was busy from open to close, every day.

The girls' father loaded the delivery van with another order of flower arrangements for the second of four weddings. Weekday mornings and Saturday, Mr. Cho delivered flowers. Then weekday afternoons, he was behind his desk in the office above the flower shop attending to the accounting of his wife's store and several other local businesses.

****

Granddad Salas was in his woodshop with Grandpa Molosky, to build their booth for the fairgrounds…in the shape of a giant red pepper. Both men were covered in sawdust and spotted with red paint from the spray gun.

In the house, Lena and Joey stood sullen and their father was resigned. He had left his post as pharmacist with his assistant for a few hours, to help his parents with their entry into the parade, but hadn't bargained for his mother's rather strange advertising approach.

Grandma Salas had made three costumes. She zipped, snapped and pinned one for her son, and one each for her grandchildren to wear in the parade. She stood back to see if there was any further adjustments she needed to make to fit her creations. "Now give me a smile. All of you must smile in the parade."

Mr. Salas and his children knew with certain dread that when they appeared in the parade, wearing the costumes that had taken Grandma Salas so long to craft - the chances of having their public appearance forgotten – was pretty well zip, to none.

****

"I can't possibly stir any longer. I've lost all feeling in both of my arms." Her head of dark curls drooped in the heat. Hanna Gaikis felt like Cinderella and decided that she really would have preferred to have been born into royalty. At twelve, Hanna was not sure what she wanted to do after high school graduation but she knew it would have to be something that didn't require any physical effort.

"Just keep switching arms." Hanna's mother was in no mood for complaining. Mrs. Gaikis had worked for ten days in a row.

Hanna and her mother stirred the ingredients in a steady parade of bowls that contained various types of batter. Over the course of the past two days, mother and daughter made eighty dozen - scones, muffins and cookies to serve with flavored iced teas, iced coffees and lemonade at the Tumbleweed Café's fairgrounds booth. Even as busy as they were, the kitchen of the Tumbleweed Café was quieter now and easier to work in with Mrs. Carter out of the way.

Mr. Carter had arrived in his truck filled with lumber for Mrs. Carter's patio-tea-house styled booth. No one was prepared to point out to Mrs. Carter – and certainly not Mr. Carter – that the money she spent for her space at the fairgrounds was far more than she would ever get in profits.

When finished, the patio would be draped with white canvas for shade. For the deck Mrs. Carter had ordered two dozen small, round white metal tables. Each table had two matching chairs. The tables would have red and white striped, canvas covers.

All the plastic plates, cups and cutlery were also bright red. In the center of each table Mrs. Carter planned a bright blue vase with one fresh red carnation and one fresh white daisy. No rodeo fairgrounds had seen anyone with quite the same flair for the impractical as Mrs. Carter.

CHAPTER TWELVE
We Gotta Find a Body

June 22…

No one seemed to notice that Ms. Perez was not in town. No one that is except Hanna, Leif, Stephen, Gordon, Joey, Mia and Sonia. The young detectives had only managed to meet once as an entire group. With the rodeo added to their regular duties it was more of a drain on their free time. Gordon told Mia everything he could remember that he overheard at the Sheriff's office. She added it to her notes and then passed it on.

The kids watched the changing locations of Ms. Perez's parked Jeep, like a lame game of musical cars. The first day it was parked in front of the sheriff's office. The second day it was back in front of cottage number twelve at Deer Lodge Motel. The third day the Jeep was parked between the newspaper office and the library. The fourth day it was back at the motel.

The sheriff appeared jumpy. The kids knew that soon the locals would begin to wonder why Ms. Perez was not showing up for any meals at any of the restaurants. But for the moment, Mosquito Creek residents were preoccupied with plans and activities for the parade and rodeo.

****

Gordon had a copy of the Montana Forestry Mining and Minerals Map, number 18-8580A. His dad and his grandfather had circled where each of the coal test wells were located. They both thought a news story about the abandoned wells was an excellent idea. With all of his lies and half truth's piling up like rows of brick, Gordon decided that Sonia was going to help him actually write something.

With the map safely rolled up in a cardboard tube that protruded from his backpack, Gordon left the newspaper office. He cycled to meet with the other young detectives gathering at Bitter Root Crossing.

It was just after noon when Gordon arrived. Joey sat on a large rock next to a trestle support eating a granola bar. Leif and Stephen had set up their archery target and were practicing. Hanna rested below the shade of a willow and watched them.

Gordon leaned his bike against the trunk of a spruce and joined the others. Joey finished his snack then unfolded a large plastic tarp the kids kept stashed behind a grouping of downed trees.

"Guess we better get started and put a plan together." Gordon looked around. "Where is Mia and Sonia?"

"They're still not here." Hanna offered.

"You're kidding." Gordon rolled his eyes. "Those two are always slow. And it was Sonia who wanted me to get this map right away."

In the distance they heard Mia call. "We're c-o-m-i-n-g!" A minute later the two girls peddled passed the group seated on the tarp and dropped their bikes on the ground by the archery target. They rushed to sit on a space left at one corner of the tarp. Both girls wheezed in gasps from their hard peddle to the meeting place.

"Sorry." Sonia panted. "Mia was on time. I was late. I had to help with Sunday school today." She took a breath. "It wasn't my turn, Anna didn't show up."

Everyone was very interested. Stephen spoke first. "Really? My dad said that the Knudsen's seemed to be making themselves quite scarce since that Ms. Perez arrived in town."

"My mom said the family is acting even more aloof too." Hanna added. "And – Mrs. Carter was real miffed because she had to play bridge with a substitute partner. Mrs. Knudsen's secretary called at the last minute to tell Mrs. Carter that she couldn't make it."

Sonia started thinking.

Mia offered. "Well my mom said that by now Mrs. Knudsen had placed her bouquet order for the ranch's presentations to the winning rodeo competitors. And Douglas and Kevin Knudsen are usually annoying everyone with daily phone calls, but this rodeo year, everyone at the ranch has been real quiet."

Sonia jumped in. "Gordon, is there anything else that you can remember from the conversation you listened to at the sheriff's office?"

He quickly thought through the eight nerve wracking minutes he had risked, eves dropping and shook his head. "Not really. I'm pretty sure I didn't forget anything important. But, who else besides us and the Knudsen's would be interested in how Ms. Perez is doing with her investigation? I mean really?"

They all looked at each other. Joey shrugged. "Do you suppose the Knudsen's would do anything to Ms. Perez?"

Stephen shook his head. "They might like to but they really need her to finish up her investigation and close the file. The Knudsen's need to get that death certificate and a sign-off cause my dad says they can't inherit anything without it."

Mia flipped to the page in her notebook where she wrote Gordon's information. "There is definitely something here. We were right to suspect foul play. Even the insurance investigator is looking deeper. Everyone at the ranch is watching Ms. Perez but she is a stranger so maybe we can find clues where she can't."

"If the Knudsen's zapped both Zara Grant and her grandfather, we need to be so-very-careful." Mia continued. "Cause they aren't going to let a few kids keep them from inheriting several million dollars."

"There are seven of us here, Mia." Gordon scowled. "They can't make all of us disappear."

"Don't be too sure about what desperate people might try." Leif cautioned.

"Leif has a point." Sonia faced her friends. "We're snooping where some very nasty people - have a multi-million dollar reason - to keep their secret hidden. And if we're right, they have already gotten rid of two members of their own family!"

Mia turned back through the pages of her note pad. "I'm not sure where we can go with the poison theory for Mr. Grant's heart attack. Mr. Hawkins didn't see anything unusual with any of the leaves Sonia and I took from those plants at the inn's green house."

"I had to be so careful. Mr. Hawkins was real curious about why I had collected so many different leaves. I told him I was interested in allergy information. I lied about thinking of a special career in medicine to research herbs that could be either toxic or beneficial."

"He did tell me about plants that have both beneficial and toxic properties. Apparently rhubarb is one. The stalk is beneficial but the leaves can be toxic."

Hanna spoke up. "Could a rhubarb leaf cause a heart attack?"

"I don't know." Mia shrugged. "I didn't want to push Mr. Hawkins much more."

Gordon unrolled the map. "We can't really do much investigating about Mr. Grant's death yet, but we can check out some of these wells. Three of the test wells were explored by two different mining companies on ranch property fairly close to the inn."

"There is one here." He pointed with a small stick. "It's only eight miles west of the inn and there are two more. The second one is here, eleven miles west and north of the inn. And the third well is just twelve miles from the inn and one mile due north of the second well."

"Don't you think we should check the wells that are furthest from the inn?" Stephen asked. "There are five wells marked. Three are on the ranch but the other two are fairly close together further along the other side of this lower ridge in the foothills. If I was going to stash a body, I'd want it to be a much greater distance away than eight miles and I sure wouldn't want it on my property."

"The time is important." Hanna reminded the group. "The night Zara Grant disappeared her great aunt was at the inn the entire day. My mom remembered the afternoon Zara went out for a ride because she wished she could have gone with her. Mrs. Knudsen was in a bad mood and critical of everything that mom had done that day in the dining room."

"That means that Mrs. Knudsen needed the help from one or both of her sons to make Zara disappear. If either Douglas, or Kevin or both flew from Minnesota to Montana, they needed an alibi. And - they had to arrange for Zara to disappear as swiftly as possible so they wouldn't be missed."

Mia checked their copy of the newspaper feature story. "Mr. Sullivan wrote that, 'just over an hour after Zara road out, her horse returned to the barn without her'. That wasn't much time."

They all crowded around the map. With his finger, Gordon traced an invisible line from the inn to the first well location. He took the pencil from Mia, made a mark then handed it back. "The ranch is here. The entire area along this stretch of foothills is heavily treed. There are specific deer paths that cut all through this area, which is the best way to go on horseback."

"If we add the most time it might take for a rider to head out on a leisurely trot from the inn, to the galloping return of a startled horse, my guess is that any one of the three wells that are on ranch property would be a perfect place to hide a body."

"It might have even been made to look like an accident." Offered Mia. "Just in case a search party found her…" Mia suddenly went silent as an even more chilling reality presented itself. "Poor Zara. She may have even been thrown down one of those wells alive."

The others were quiet for a moment staring at the map in front of them.

"I remember my dad and grandfather going out every day, nights too for seven days in a row with a search party of several hundred people." Gordon added. "They used tracking dogs and Zara's Scottie but found no trace at all. I'm sure my dad would have thought of those well locations and they would have been searched."

Hanna remembered. "I've seen other maps just like this. Before my mom was fired, I was at the inn with my mom every day after Zara disappeared. There were people all over the place. Mr. Grant was a wreck and Mrs. Knudsen shut herself in her room. Maps that looked like this one were tacked up on the walls of the dining room. No one mentioned any wells. They may not have thought of them. Sometimes under stress we miss important details."

"It's getting late." Joey checked his watch. "If we're gonna look for each of these three wells today we need to get started."

"He's right." Mia looked at her watch too. "It's already one-twenty. We have dinner earlier on Sundays."

"Are we riding our bikes?" Hanna asked. "Those deer paths are pretty steep."

"We pretty well have to." Sonia made a face thinking of the narrow, steep and winding paths in the wooded foothills they needed to explore. "I thought of borrowing some horses but the ranch is the only place that has enough for all of us to…"

Gordon interrupted Sonia. "We only have one map. The seven of us can't split up and go to each location. And - only two or three of us at a time should go for a ride so it won't create suspicion."

Stephen made a decision. "And, if we're trying not to attract attention then different people should ask for the horses, except for Gordon because he has the map. I think Gordon, me, and Hanna should bike to the ranch. If anyone asks, we might be able to use the scavenger hunt story again but Mia, Sonia and Joey have already been at the ranch with that excuse. Mia's right we're wasting what's left of the day."

The junior detectives disbanded. Gordon folded the map and tucked it into his shirt. Leif put away his brother's bow. Hanna followed

93

Stephen walking their bikes under the trestle bridge with Gordon lagging a little behind.

On the other side of the bridge a narrow gravel road led back to the main road that followed Lost Creek to Mosquito Creek Inn. The ranch's stock manager Leo Potter knew of the relationship Gordon had to the missing heiress. Because Mr. Potter considered the McKenna kids ranch family, Gordon knew that if the stock manager was around Gordon could take any horse he wanted out to exercise.

Since this was a spur-of-the-moment alteration of their original plan to search on their bikes, Gordon hoped that Mr. Potter was working. If he wasn't in the horse barn, then maybe whoever was on duty might accept an I.O.U. as payment.

Stephen held Gordon's bike as he went into the barn to ask for Leo Potter. In less than two minutes, Gordon reappeared and waved to his friends.

Mr. Potter was short but very muscular with thinning, dark curly hair. He had a wide mouth filled with large white teeth. "So you want to go for a ride." He looked Stephen and Hanna over. "When was the last time you two rode a horse?"

Then he looked at Hanna again. "Say you look very familiar."

"I'm Hanna Gaikis. My mother Susan Gaikis was the inn's restaurant manager for two years. I rode some when my mom worked here."

"Of course. Your mom left soon after I came. My gosh, you're almost all grown. I haven't seen you since you were what five? I don't go into the Tumbleweed Café. So I only see your mom now and then, usually at the post office."

Stephen volunteered. "I haven't ridden for quite a while either but I have ridden, sir."

Mr. Potter laughed. "Thanks son but no one calls me sir or Mr. Potter. Just so happens I got two great mares and a gelding that need some exercise. Follow me."

The kids helped with the blankets and the bridles but Mr. Potter insisted on adjusting the saddles himself. "Don't want someone slipping and ending upside-down. That can really spook a horse. Now when you come back, if you don't see me, just go ahead and take off the tack then brush them down in their stalls. Got that?"

The three riders nodded then pointed their mounts west toward the heavily wooded foothills.

CHAPTER THIRTEEN
This Just Gets Worse

June 23…

They found a body.

The discovery of a human skeleton in coal test well M67 caused the most amazing blizzard of shock - felt far beyond the town of Mosquito Creek.

News of the discovery was broadcasted by Montana television and radio stations. Overnight, national networks picked up on the find for their early morning broadcast.

When Ms. Perez stepped off the Greyhound bus she had taken to return to Mosquito Creek from Helena, she had not yet heard of this latest development because… About the time Ms. Perez was driving back to Helena in her rental car - Gordon, Hanna and Stephen had begun pulling away the branches and debris from the opening of the first well they checked on their map. Still on ranch land it was the farthest away from the inn, by almost twelve miles.

And about the time the Ms. Perez was refilling the gas tank of her rental car – Stephen's flashlight illuminated human, skeletal remains. Stephen spotted the right hand first and was so spooked he nearly passed out and dropped his flashlight into the well opening.

Then, about the time that Ms. Perez returned her rental car and made her first phone call for a return ride to Mosquito Creek - the sheriff's office had emptied out. All available on duty and off duty police officers as well as every volunteer fireman, and forestry personnel headed for the well location just below Pioneer Ridge.

After forty minutes of dialing the sheriff's office number with no answer, Ms. Perez caught a Greyhound bus back to Mosquito Creek. Another forty-five minutes later the bus stopped at the Coleman-Lansing hotel. She hoped to avoid being recognized, so she wore sunglasses and a scarf to that covered her hair. She didn't need to worry, all focus of the entire county was miles away.

A few steps from the bus stop Ms. Perez ducked between two buildings to remove her scarf. She tied it to the strap of her overnight bag then stepped back onto the sidewalk to make her way to the sheriff's office. As she walked, she tried to think of an explanation for the overnight bag if she was spotted by any of the local people she had interviewed.

The late morning sun was already intense. When she turned the corner to the sheriff's office, another blast of heat came from the parking area beside the office. The lot was alive with arriving vehicles. Puzzled, Ms. Perez ran up the front steps and through the narrow double doors into the office. Two groups of people, some in uniform some in street clothes, were talking on phones in the outer office area.

A third group of people had assembled around the conference table in the sheriff's office. All four phone lines to the telephone on the desk of the office manager glowed red but Mrs. Spear was not answering any of the lines. She was on the dispatch radio with the headset on, taking notes. Mrs. Spear caught sight of Ms. Perez and then pointed over her head toward Sheriff Howard's office. Ms. Perez left her bags on the floor beside Mrs. Spears' desk on her way to the open office door.

A tense discussion was already in progress.

"We may be getting ahead of ourselves at the moment." Sheriff Howard tapped the eraser end of his pencil on the tabletop. "We have the remains of a person who was just over five feet tall but we don't yet know if the skeleton was that of a male or female." The sheriff looked across the room to the row of windows on the east wall "I'm sorry Park."

Ms. Perez hadn't noticed the newspaper editor. Mr. Sullivan stood by the window, away from the small round table of people. The editor's expression was grim. His skin color was as grey as ash. There were deep, dark circles under his normally cheery eyes.

"Bella." Sheriff Howard stood then reached out and took her by the arm then led her to join everyone at the table. "Let me introduce you. Let's see, you met Paul McKenna with Federal Parks, this is Dr. Ralph Howes who also acts as our coroner. Over here is Paula Lincoln, FBI Community Liaison out of the Helena office and Frank Whitehead, who heads up the local office for Montana State Patrol. Everyone, this is the Mid-Western Insurance Investigator I told you about, Ms. Bella Perez."

"All the other people out there with Mayor Peters" the sheriff pointed to the open door, "are more FBI, highway patrol and forestry." The sheriff nodded toward the window. "Park Sullivan, our newspaper editor you met last week."

Ms. Perez worked her way around the table and shook hands with each of the people the sheriff introduced. When she got to an empty chair, she hesitated. "Excuse me for a moment. I'm going to get my briefcase."

When she returned to her seat the sheriff had picked up the map that had been spread out across the table. Ms. Perez and the others watched as he pinned the very detailed topographic map of Powell County onto his office cork board. The map covered up several wanted posters, faxes and memos.

"This office owes you an apology Ms. Perez." To the others in the room the sheriff explained. "We were supposed to give this lady a ride back to town from Helena. To be honest, in all the excitement we forgot about her. However, I'm glad to see that you were resourceful enough to return without our assistance."

"We didn't forget you completely though. I let everyone know Ms. Perez that you were searching for physical evidence that would connect one or more of our suspects to events that lead up to the day that Zara Grant disappeared and possibly to the day that Khors Grant died."

Ms. Perez was caught off guard and quite overwhelmed at the sudden attention focused on Mosquito Creek. She would have preferred to complete her findings quietly on her own. She decided not to wait for an explanation for the gathering of so many local, state, and federal official law enforcement. "So, what's going on?" She asked cautiously.

The sheriff filled her in. "Late yesterday afternoon, three local kids who were horseback riding along a deer path just below Pioneer Ridge" The sheriff pointed to a place on the map. "Found the human skeletal remains of what Dr. Howes believes -without further testing - to be that of a young female."

The insurance investigator was caught completely by surprise and her expression showed it.

The sheriff continued. "One of the kids who made the discovery was Gordon McKenna. Gordon is the park ranger's son and our newspaper editor's grandson. The kids went up there to do some sort of research on the abandoned coal and water wells around here for a news article, or something. Who knows, kids are kids."

"Anyway, this well is just ten miles inside the north-west border of the Grant Ranch property line and twelve miles from the inn. Mrs. Knudsen is furious about this discovery. According to her it intrudes on the privacy of her important guests."

The sheriff pointed to the doctor. "So, Doc Howes was just about to leave to meet with our local dentist Clark Putman, to finish a preliminary examination of the remains. FBI Agent Lincoln has what is left of the fragments of clothing that was still clinging to the skeleton."

The sheriff looked at Mr. Sullivan again then back to the table. "So if our dentist and our doctor need any additional assistance the FBI is here."

Dr. Howes checked the time then stood up. "I better go. I had arranged to meet Clark Putman at the dental clinic six minutes ago." He waived to everyone as he hurried out of the office door.

The sheriff sat down at the table again. "That's pretty much what has happened here, in a nut-shell so to speak. Ms. Perez, you were away a day longer than you thought you might be, did you have any luck?"

Ms. Perez was still floundering from the news of the discovery of a skeleton. She tried to collect her thoughts. She looked directly at the forest ranger, Paul McKenna. "Since one of the boys who discovered the body was your son, he and his friends must be very shaken-up. I'm sorry."

"Shaken doesn't even begin to describe how this has affected each of the kids. My son Gordon went horseback riding with two friends, Stephen Anderlund and Hanna Gaikis. But their nice ride took a very nasty turn."

Ms. Perez nodded, checked her notes then felt she could brief the people assembled in the room. "Billings was a dead end. I managed to trace Kevin Knudsen from Rochester, Minnesota to Billings, Montana but could not find any record of either a car rental or a hotel stay, at least not with any of the chain hospitality lodgings."

She hesitated slightly when she noticed the FBI Agent Paula Lincoln had a small tape recorder. "I…checked with local authorities for any known associations and the Chamber of Commerce, for any possible business dealings. But I found nothing."

From her briefcase, Ms. Perez pulled out a small map of her own. "From Billings I drove to Great Falls. This is a huge state by the way. I got lost twice." Those listening at the table smiled. "I thought I had discovered something in Great Falls. One of the former managers of RentaCar-USA was sent to prison in Idaho for illegal gambling and company embezzlement."

"What took an extra day was my side trip to Idaho, via a Great Falls commuter plane." Everyone at the table was paying close attention. "Mrs. Knudsen's oldest son Douglas flew to Great Falls twice from Minnesota."

"Apparently Douglas Knudsen likes to gamble too. He and the former RentaCar manager," she checked her notes, "a Roger Winton, were involved in several betting schemes. But only Mr. Winton was ever directly implicated. The gambling was a surprise the police discovered, only after Mr. Winton was charged with stealing funds from the office he formerly managed."

"Mr. Winton was not very cooperative but he let enough slip for me to believe that Douglas Knudsen was offered the use of a rental car *off-the-books* so that he could travel undetected. I believe he came to Mosquito Creek."

FBI Agent Paula Lincoln looked puzzled. "I can see where you might be going with this Ms. Perez but if Douglas Knudsen didn't want any connection between himself and secret trips to Mosquito Creek, why would he use his own name and his credit card to book a regular flight from his home town of Rochester to Great Falls?"

The insurance investigator nodded. "My theory on that is that Douglas wanted his trips to appear as if they were normal, legitimate business trips, with nothing to hide." She looked to Sheriff Howard then back to the FBI agent.

Ms. Perez was nervous but tried to press her point. "The sheriff and I held separate interviews with Zigvarta Knudsen, both of her sons and their wives. The sons each insisted that even before their second cousin Zara disappeared and their uncle Khors died, they were researching business opportunities in Montana."

While the insurance investigator was making her point, Mayor Peters had quietly slipped into the room. He tiptoed over to where the newspaper editor stood alone by the window. A second FBI agent had followed the mayor into the room. He took a place just inside the door.

The phones had been ringing so much over the morning that when it rang again no one paid any attention until Mrs. Spear appeared at the door. She looked directly at her boss. "Sheriff, I have Dr. Howes on the line. You might want to have the phone on speaker so everyone can hear what he discovered."

The sheriff nodded to the mayor. "Go ahead and press the yellow button on my desk phone mayor, then everyone will be able to hear."

The mayor pushed the button to open the speaker line.

Mrs. Spear returned to her desk to transfer the doctor's call.

The mayor remained standing by the phone as the sheriff addressed the doctor.

"Ralph, can ya hear me?"

"Yeah, no problem."

"I have you on speaker so you can talk to everyone. What'ya got?"

"My preliminary examination is that the remains of the body found in the coal well, is that of a young woman between the age of twenty and thirty. The bones in the hands are completely formed, that only occurs after the age of eighteen. The pelvic bones confirm that the remains are female and the young woman had at least one full term pregnancy."

"There is evidence of severe blunt force trauma to one side of the skull. I don't know yet if that was as a result of the fall down the well or if the young woman met with fowl-play and someone hit her then pushed her into the well. However, I can assure you the remains of the female skeleton the kids discovered, is not that of Zara Grant."

"Clark, will be on the phone and back in here any moment. I think he knows the identity of our skeleton. He took one look at the teeth, shouted '*hot-cow-doo!*' then ran out of here."

"When I looked at the lower jaw, I saw where four wisdom teeth had been extracted because the openings in the bone had not healed and…"

Doctor Howes was interrupted.

The listeners in the sheriff's office heard a door close. They could hear the voices of Dr. Howes and the dentist Clark Putman, whispering. Then the doctor came back to his receiver. "I'm putting my phone on speaker too. Putman located the records he needed. Clark knows who the kids found."

Dr. Putman spoke. "Can everyone there hear me clearly?"

The sheriff spoke for everyone assembled in his office. Mrs. Spear stood in the doorway. All the deputies and several others in the outer office gathered just behind her.

"Is the mayor still there? Clark asked.

Mayor Peters, spoke for himself. "Yes Clark I'm still here. Go ahead."

The dentist continued. "One week before Frances Cooper left town, I had extracted all four of her wisdom teeth. She was twenty-six and had suffered with a mouth full of overcrowded teeth and the wisdom teeth had become impacted."

"The remains of the young woman found in the well is the mother of Philip Cooper Peters. Philip's mother didn't desert him at all. She died."

CHAPTER FOURTEEN
Shadow And Light

June 25…

It was parade day.

However never, in the history of the annual rodeo, had the day of the parade dawned with the entire population of Mosquito Creek, talking about anything, but the kick-off to its annual rodeo.

The atmosphere between the town and the ranch was a bubbling pot of vinegar. Suspicions and theories swirled in a dust storm of open speculation. With the discovery of Frances Cooper's skeleton, it became apparent that the formally quiet town of Mosquito Creek had more than one mystery to solve.

Philip Cooper Peters had no memory of his mother, so the mayor and his wife decided that the remains of Frances Cooper would be interred the following week at a private ceremony after the rodeo was over. Philip called the mayor and his wife, Dad and Mom. He could point to the photograph of his mother that Mrs. Peters enlarged then framed for Philip's room.

As wise as Philip was he still had some limits. Mayor and Mrs. Peters were thankful that Philip's syndrome caused him to live mostly in the moment. It spared him the pain that might have been life altering to a child who was more aware.

Traditionally, the Mayor of Mosquito Creek judged each parade entry. Mayor Peters always took Philip with him for this official occasion. Each year, the mayor and his youngest son inspected the parade floats, the bands, decorated horses and livestock entries. They always made the winning selections together.

Mayor Peters, his wife and Philip sat with Montana's Governor, his family, State Legislators, Senators, Congressmen and other invited dignitaries. From their vantage on raised bleachers, they could see the parade starting point.

In past years, the rodeo was hosted by Grant Ranch. A member of the Grant family acted as parade coordinator and grand marshal. After Kohrs Grant died, his sister took over. But, abruptly, just a few days before the parade Mrs. Knudsen sent word that she was not well and that her son's had other pressing business matters to address.

The parade's final details might well have been in question. However, during the rodeo meeting when Mr. Potter the ranch stock manager presented Mrs. Knusden's regrets, he volunteered as a replacement for grand marshal.

The rodeo committee was so relieved to have this burden lifted they quickly agreed that Mr. Potter was a logical choice. He was a little out of his element with the sudden attention and social responsibility but he had the additional input and organizational assistance of Mrs. Carter, who intended to ensure her float was at the front of the parade, right behind the high school marching band.

When the parade rounded the first corner onto the main street into town, Mr. Potter was front and center. The new parade marshal rode his dapple-gray, prize winning cutting horse, Avalanche. The blanket edges, saddle and bridle were polished, black leather. Mr. Potter wore black pants with a gray suede leather shirt and a gray felt cowboy hat. Horse and rider were a fine, impressive beginning to the parade.

Sonia tapped her grandpa's arm. "I've never seen Mr. Potter so dressed up." They watched as Leo Potter took off his hat to wave at the crowd that lined Main Street.

"Me either." Grandpa Molosky was just as surprised. "A stranger might think this year's parade marshal owned Grant Ranch."

The Deer Lodge Marching Band followed. Their dress uniforms were two-toned green. Next, appeared a circular all white, lattice wood gazebo, that turned slowly on the back of a large flatbed trailer. Mrs. Carter and her two young sons were dressed in pioneer style costumes. They waved from inside the gazebo. A continuous banner that wrapped around the entire base of the trailer, advertised the Tumbleweed Café and the *Hoof* Steak House.

"Mrs. Carter should be in Hollywood, Dad." Philip whispered.

Mayor Peters laughed out loud. He nodded as he took his young son's hand and patted it. "You're so right."

Next came all of the rodeo entrants on their horses. The cowboys wore their finest complete with prize-winning silver belt buckles, hand tooled leather boots, custom made leather and suede pants, jackets and embroidered shirts. Their horses pranced, and high-stepped with the finest of leather and silver trimmed bridles and saddles.

Parade spectators broke into spontaneous applause as Silas Tate appeared. He walked beside his prizewinning pig, Tulip. The pig was fitted with a saddle and bridle. Riding in the saddle was one of Mr. Tate's young turkeys in a barely visible wire basket. The turkey wore a small cowboy hat and with a scarf tied around its neck.

A tractor backfired as it came around the corner pulling a giant taco. Inside the taco was Joey Salas dressed as a lettuce leaf with his sister Lena dressed as an onion. Beside the taco walked their father dressed as a large tomato. Driving the tractor was Granddad Salas, almost unrecognizable as a cob of corn.

The mayor could hardly wait. He knew he'd get years of razzing the local pharmacist, long after the 1997 parade was a distant memory. The entries this year were unusually creative and decidedly entertaining.

A tall, bushy blue spruce tree rounded the corner next. Stephen could just barely see through the branches to drive the riding lawn mower. Leif stood among the branches by the trunk of the tree helping to hold it secure and making sure none of the guide wires broke. On the top of the tree was a three-foot silver star that twinkled with lights that spelled Anderlund's Market. Hanging from several branches were large papier-mâché decorations in the shape of the organic produce and of the natural foods sold in the market.

Philip stood and waved. The mayor shook his head laughing. The thick tree looked like it was gliding down the street on its own.

Behind the tree came another tractor decorated to look like a large flower box. In the flower box was five foot silk leaves. Mr. Cho sat among the leaves on the seat of the tractor. The flower box pulled a large wagon. Inside the wagon were four oversized flower pots made from cardboard with painted designs. Mia and Niki, each dressed as a daisy, sat inside one of the flower pots at the back of the wagon.

In the flower pots at the front of the wagon sat their mother, who was dressed as an iris and their aunt dressed as a pansy. Mia and Niki tossed handfuls of carnation heads out into the crowd.

In the wake of the mysteries that Mosquito Creek needed to solve, the timing of this parade was perfect. If only for a few hours, the town needed to be distracted by activities that were not so bleak.

The parade's end destination was the rodeo fairgrounds. There, the prizeentrants gathered in rows in the same order as they had appeared in the parade. The crowd of locals, visitors and tourists all followed the end of the parade to the grounds, where they reassembled in the bleachers.

Mayor Peters and Philip discussed the parade entrants and made their prize winning selections. On the bandstand in front of the bleachers the mayor took the microphone to make his formal announcement of the prize winners.

An honorable mention was presented first to Mr. Tate, his pig and the cowboy-turkey. Everyone laughed and applauded. His prize was a new lariat. Mr. Tate tipped his hat to Mayor Peters then presented his prize of the coiled new rope to Philip.

"First prize for the 1997outstanding float with $500 cash prize or equivalent merchandise at Trask Hardware - goes to Rosa Salas for her giant taco. With, a special honorable mention going to her particularly talented red tomato!" The mayor found the pharmacist in the crowd and pointed. There was more laughter and applause.

The mayor continued. "A second prize of $300 cash or the equivalent in dinner out at Les Tres Luna Restaurant, goes to Su Cho of *Petals Flower Shoppe*." There were more cheers and more applause.

"Third and last prize of $150 cash, or equivalent in movie enjoyment goes to Stephen and Leif Anderlund of Anderlund's Market. Their walking tree was very unique"

The crowd whistled and applauded.

Carl hugged his boys.

Leif and Stephen were astonished and thrilled. "Yes!" They congratulated each other with a high-five before joining the other prize winners on the band stand.

CHAPTER FIFTEEN
Storm Clouds Return

June 26…

The town of Mosquito Creek was really over stuffed.

There were hundreds of visiting cowboys. The rodeo competitors didn't pay much attention to the newspaper headlines. To them it was just another media event that had nothing to do with their job, which was the rodeo circuit prize money.

Added to the cowboy numbers, were hundreds of tourists and out of town friends and family for the several June weddings. And then with the remains of Frances Cooper discovered, most of Powell County became a virtual salad of law enforcement people.

As well, two national networks had slipped in a dozen reporters with film crew, completely undetected. Their unmarked motor homes and trailers both small and large assembled at the Arrowstone Camp Grounds, a mile south of town.

The invading media crew wore vacation clothing and carried small handheld cameras. They looked like every other tourist. Not even Mr. Anderlund was aware that members of the major networks were on the streets and in the crowds of Mosquito Creek.

****

Neither Hanna nor her mother had been able to enjoy any significant time off for two weeks. Hanna had even slept over night at the Carter house on four separate occasions. With a greater number of visitors than in previous years, Mrs. Carter opened the Tumbleweed Café an hour earlier and stayed open two hours later. The serving and cook staff worked an extra shift everyday trying to serve hungry diners at the fairgrounds and the restaurant.

The crowd pressure forced Mr. Carter to open each day for lunch and continue to serve full meals until midnight. He cleaned, he made salads, he served drinks, and food. Mr. Carter's plans for slack-time with his old rodeo pals was, limited to short visits from behind his bar.

Joey and his younger sister Lena fell into bed each night just as exhausted as their father and grandparents. Joey swept the floors, brought sodas and iced tea, helped at the cash register and was another pair of legs for his grandfather and Mr. Molosky, who was also pressed into service. His sister cleared and wiped the tables and helped her grandma chop the fresh ingredients Granddad Salas needed when he cooked.

Grandma and Granddad Salas opened their Mexican food restaurant one hour earlier at ten in the morning then stayed open until twelve each night. The family had to operate the restaurant short staffed because half their regular help worked in their booth at the fairgrounds.

Their father's notions and pharmacy store was a constant flow of sales for sunscreen, sunglasses, candy, cosmetics, allergy and headache remedies. For the long weekend of the rodeo, Mr. Salas opened an hour earlier and remained open until the fireworks at eleven every evening.

Mia and her sister Niki almost slept at their mother's flower shop. They spent hours at a time sitting on tall wooden stools cutting flower stems and ribbon. There were moments when Mia didn't think she could feel her legs any more.

****

Stephen and Leif hardly saw the rodeo. Their stepmother and stepsister were occupied with their booth at the fairgrounds. Their father divided his time between the market and his new wife's booth.

Mr. Anderlund and his boys had opened the market for another day of high activity. He had readjusted the last of the three wooden blinds that hung over the front windows, when he spotted two vehicles slow down then pull into his parking lot.

He looked over to where Stephen was cleaning out the birds' cage. "Our day is starting already." He pointed to the window. "Is it just my imagination or is there about double the number of people here for the rodeo this year than last year?" Mr. Anderlund counted out the change for his till.

Leif pushed a large broom down the aisle just in front of the checkout counter. "It's the body. People are curious about the skeleton Stephen found." He looked over to his brother. "How many times in the past three days have you been asked a hundred stupid questions about finding what was left of Frances Cooper?"

Stephen shrugged. "I don't know. Enough to make me wish I was actually one of these goofy birds."

Mr. Anderlund winked at Leif then addressed his older son. "Well perhaps Mrs. Salas could create a disguise for you with feathers. She made her entire family into vegetables."

When the customers walked into the store, Leif was laughing so hard he got the hiccups.

****

Sonia finished with the vacuum upstairs. Next she had to clean the bathrooms. She called her brother Eric who took the vacuum to sweep the main floor. She set her sister Salina the task of pulling the sheets off of everyone's bed. As she misted the mirror over the bathroom sink, Sonia heard her other brother Marc clink dishes as he emptied the dishwasher.

Mrs. Molosky had settled in behind her desk in her real estate office above the garage. Earlier she had mowed the grass in the back yard. Philip Peters was attempting to help by raking up the cut grass but Joker kept running off with the plastic grass bags.

The Molosky household stirred with activity. Their entire circle of friends, were rushed and busy and every day was filled with tourist and rodeo obligations. Sonia sat on the edge of the bath tub absently swirling the cleaning sponge across the rows of tile.

Sonia was more troubled by Mrs. Knudsen and her sons than ever. She had been so certain that they would find Zara but the body they discovered was Philip's mother. So where was Zara Grant? How many murders had Mrs. Knudsen and her sons committed?

She thought about the front page story Mr. Sullivan ran about Frances Cooper's disappearance. No one had known much about her.

Mrs. Cooper had arrived in town in the spring of 1986, hidden in the back of Mr. Anderlund's produce truck. When he returned from the market distribution center in Great Falls, Mr. Anderlund had no idea he was hauling anything more than onions, peppers and tomatoes until he stopped at the back of the Les Tres Luna Restaurant, to deliver their order.

The destitute widow was already expecting a baby when she arrived in Mosquito Creek, but from the start, she worked diligently. She formed her own small business cleaning offices and restaurants at night. Then she cleaned the cottages at the Deer Lodge Motel every morning. After Philip was born everywhere she went, Frances always took him with her.

Suddenly, Sonia jumped up and ran to her room. She pulled the pink backpack out from under her bed. Inside she retrieved the 1990 calendar. On the back of the calendar was a bonus page that showed all of the months for 1991 in smaller blocks.

Flipping back and forth, she wondered...

"What are you doing with that out?" Salina stood in the open bedroom doorway with a stricken look on her face.

Sonia jumped. Then realized she hadn't been discovered. "Don't do that! You almost gave me a stroke!"

"I gave *you* a stroke? Aunt Monica is just down stairs and Mom's in her office. You're very lucky it was only me!"

Sonia's heart rate had returned to near normal. "I only had the old calendar out. The rest of the papers are still in Mia's back pack. I was checking out the time between when Zara Grant disappeared, then when Frances Cooper disappeared, cause now we know she didn't leave town."

"Frances Cooper cleaned offices, some businesses and the Deer Lodge Motel. Mia thinks Mrs. Cooper found something or may have seen something or may have over heard something in one of the places where she cleaned. She and Philip lived in the last cabin at the motel and she never locked her door. So anyone could have walked in on her at anytime day or night."

Sonia put down the calendar then rummaged for a copy of another news article. Salina stayed in the doorway as lookout. Sonia found what she needed.

"It says here that Philip was wrapped in a sleeping bag and left at the front door of the mayor's house sound asleep. The note that was pinned to the zipper was typed on the bottom half of a torn piece of stationery that matched the paper from Clausen's Insurance."

She looked at her younger sister. "Mom said that Frances cleaned Mr. Clausen's office. Mom also told me that Jim Clausen sold his business then moved to Oregon to go into a construction business with a college friend."

Sonia reached for the 1990 calendar again. "Okay. Zara Grant went missing in mid August. Two months later in October, Kohrs Grant died of a heart attack." She flipped to the back page. "The following March 1991, Mrs. Cooper supposedly skipped town, seven months after Zara disappeared. Then three months after Florence Cooper disappeared, this Mr. Clausen moved away. That's a lot of major, stuff for a small place like Mosquito Creek."

Salina tried to keep track of all the people in her head. "So now you think Mrs. Cooper and Zara Grant and Zara's grandfather - were all murdered by - this Mr. Clausen?"

Sonia nodded. "Maybe? Or we have two unrelated murders. Or, Mr. Clausen didn't really move to Oregon. Maybe he knew something and the Knudsen's did him in as well "

Salina made a face. "Sonia, that could be - four dead people!"

"I know. I hav'ta call another team meeting. This is getting more complicated. We expected to find Zara's Grant's body in one of those wells, not Florence Cooper! That means that Zara's body is still out there, somewhere."

Salina pulled back with a jerk horrified at the thought. "Those other wells that Gordon had marked on the map were searched but they didn't find another body." Salina came closer to Sonia and lowered her voice. "Zara Grant may have been eaten up completely by a mountain lion."

"I hope not. But my first theory was correct - sort of. I just didn't count on any other victims. I believe Zara Grant's body is waiting to be found, out there." Sonia pointed in the direction of the ranch and the foothills. "And I think we can find her."

"You really can't be serious! Hanna's having nightmares about falling and falling and falling in a strange dark place. Gordon and Stephen see skeletons even in the daytime. Why don't you tell Grandpa? Let him talk to the sheriff."

"Our sheriff is surrounded by state police and federal police. His office is packed with people falling all over each other with files and papers everywhere. But guess who figured out where a murderer might easily hide a body? Me!"

"So if this Mr. Clausen person has already left town, there's no real danger. If he's dead too then that increases the danger. The Knudsen's are still here, all of them. If that insurance guy was helping the Knudsen's, and his body is in the woods in the foothills too, wow! That's a lot of people they made disappear."

Sonia put the old calendar in back then pushed the backpack under her bed. "Rats! You might be right. This could be a huge conspiracy."

****

The light dusting of rain that fell in the afternoon didn't interrupt the rodeo. The events went on as planned. A little mud added to the excitement and just about anyone who was within twenty feet of any of the bucking horses, the barrel races, the bucking bulls, the chuck wagon races, or the calf roping–was splattered with muck.

The man and the woman met secretly–out in the open.

With all of the noise and activity their presence was virtually ignored. And those few, who noticed at all, really didn't pay any attention. Their faces were familiar and so many other events distracted people from the significance of seeing anyone from the ranch.

"I thought you had buried Frances Cooper? Those kids, discovering her body makes the facts we created more difficult to sell." The woman took a bite of the burrito she bought at the Les Tres Luna booth.

"I didn't have the same kind of time to plan for Frances Cooper that I did for Zara Grant." The man sipped a large iced tea from a bright red, plastic glass.

"Well, at least you didn't dump both of them in the same place. You didn't, did you?' The woman smiled at people passing. Fine lines crinkled around her eyes. She kept her expression casual and her focus on the calf roping event. The woman finished her burrito.

Both of them carried a pass that allowed them to wander freely among the trailers and the livestock on the competitor's side of the events corral.

"No I didn't dump Frances's body where I dumped Zara. Where I left Zara, I doubt that even the Indians remember that place." The man gathered the reins to get on his horse.

The woman shaded her eyes as the sun broke through some clouds. "So you're sure those kids were only snooping around that specific well because of an article for the newspaper?"

"Yeah, it looks that way. We just need to keep up appearances for a little longer."

The man put his left boot into the stirrup then swung his right leg around and sat in the saddle in one smooth, practiced motion. He tipped his hat to the woman then rode away.

The woman looked away from the calf roping toward the Tumbleweed gazebo then changed her mind. She decided against tea and dessert in case she was cornered by Mrs. Carter and expected to explain herself.

CHAPTER SIXTEEN
The Posse Rides Again

June 27...

Once again, Sonia was convinced she had another great theory.

The Knudsens had made themselves scarce. Mrs. Knudsen and one son made only a single, short appearance at the rodeo. The latest rumor was that Mrs. Knudsen and her entire family were, soon returning to Minnesota for the rest of the summer. Leo Potter made the social rounds almost every day at the rodeo trying to relieve some of the tension between the town and the ranch.

Just a few minutes before nine, Sonia showed up at the newspaper office dragging Eric with her. Sonia had convinced her brother that Mr. Sullivan needed more people to help with this week's edition than just Gordon and his mother. Her convincing was assisted significantly by a five dollar bill.

Eric replaced Gordon in the van to help Gordon's mom. Sonia then contrived to help Gordon cover the paper delivery route down town. This time her motives weren't romantic. She needed to share her latest idea and get his cooperation.

Sonia and Gordon each pulled a long narrow flatbed wagon stacked with newspapers. They made a stop for every metal newspaper dispenser located inside the stores, restaurants and in front of businesses out on the street. Gordon counted the papers and delivered them while Sonia waited by the wagons.

Her scenario was interrupted by people stopping to buy a paper out of their hands and Gordon ducking into stores to refill the vending cases. Just outside the one-hundred-year old Black Bear Hotel, Gordon realized what Sonia was leading up to.

"Oh – no, you don't! Finding one skeleton is one too many. I'm only twelve and I'd really like to make it to thirteen."

"You said it. We know what the motive was. There's millions, and millions, and millions of dollars that the Knudsen's want very, very badly. If they made my cousin Zara disappear for that money they'll certainly make any one of us disappear for exactly the same reason."

"I'm scared too." Sonia countered, "but all of the police and all of the searching and all of the FBI still didn't figure out what we figured out or what we found. We know what happened to Philip's mom because of my theory."

"That was such a fluke! You thought Zara was in one of those wells not Mrs. Cooper. Finding the remains of Philip's mom was a surprise to us too."

"Not really." Sonia persisted, "I believe both disappearances are connected."

"That's even worse! If the Knudsen's are responsible for Zara Grant, Mr. Grant and Frances Cooper, that's t-h-r-e-e murders! Never mind how the insurance guy fits into any of this. That makes the Knudsens like, like…the…first serial killer family in history. You really wanta risk us being number four and number five – or – five and six?"

"That's not the kind of name I want to make for myself." His voice was half whisper, half hysterical panic. Gordon felt like his head would explode.

Sonia had set her jaw with that stubborn look he knew so well. She had been like that since she was five. He tried to get her to see reason.

"Mosquito Creek is crawling with all kinds of law. Sonia we all did our part. My Grandfather put your name in the paper. You saw it. It doesn't matter that everyone but the team thought you were on a crusade to protect us from dangerous, open wells. The result was the same."

She tried one last time. "Gordon this is like, so important. And, I don't want to go looking alone. There were two other wells posted on a much older map that your grandfather still has but those same wells don't show up on the newer map we used."

"That's easy." Gordon pulled his wagon down the street. "But, we don't need to be the ones who check them out! When we get back to the newspaper we can show the old map to my grandfather then tell him everything. He's cool."

Sonia pulled her wagon toward the other side of the street. She told Gordon they could finish sooner if they split up. He agreed. Sonia hurried to finish her side of down town and then rushed back to the newspaper office. She parked the wagon in the back by the loading ramp then went in through the swinging double doors.

Mr. Sullivan was in his office talking on the phone. Mrs. Sullivan was filing a stack of advertising copy. The only other staff member around was the photographer reporter Fritz Ita who had just closed the door to the dark room.

She walked over to the large wooden drafting table where the maps were stacked in no particular order. The map she was looking for was not in color like the newer maps.

The mining company that cored for minerals in 1956 was bought by a bigger mining company in 1964 that was sold an oil company in 1978. Gordon's father Paul McKenna didn't have any maps as old as the ones Mr. Sullivan had at the newspaper.

Sonia spotted the map she was looking for about five layers down. Carefully she pulled the brittle, yellowed paper out from the pile. As she studied the two well locations, she thought she knew right where they were.

Two miles further north from where Frances was found, was a natural water feature the locals called String Falls. There were three waterfalls only a few yards apart.

119

Each waterfall poured water from a single, narrow rock opening that made the water look like a long strand of white string from a distance.

Sonia rolled up the map then slid the other newer maps back on the stack. She left the newspaper office by the same door she came in. Back on her bike she hurried home to get Joker. She decided that if she was going to explore on her own, Joker was better than no company at all.

As she approached her house, she spotted her mother's van backing out of the driveway. When checked the time it was just after one o'clock. She had plenty of daylight left even if she had to explore any distance from the deer path.

Her Aunt Monica's car was still parked out front. Sonia decided not to go into the house. She wasn't prepared to answer any questions about where she was going. As far as her family knew, she and Eric were helping the Sullivan's distribute the weekly edition of the Mosquito Creek Review.

Joker was by his doghouse chewing up a cardboard box. When he saw Sonia he stopped and wagged his tail. A chunk of cardboard stuck out from one side of his mouth. She patted her knees and Joker was up and running toward her. She clipped on his leather leash then looped the end over the handlebars of her bike.

Sonia hoped Mr. Potter was not busy with the rodeo. If he wasn't at the ranch she was concerned that she might have more difficulty taking out one of the trail horses without any money. She decided that didn't matter. This was important and she was prepared to try to bike the fourteen miles to String Falls if she had to.

By twenty minutes to two Sonia was at the ranch. She peddled over to the horse barn, passed a large tour bus parked in front of the inn. Several dozen couples were escorted through the out buildings. She stood in the middle of the barn. Almost all of the stalls were occupied by some very high spirited horses. Joker strained on the leash to sniff at the horses in their stalls.

"Well, if it isn't Miss Newspaper Celebrity."

Sonia turned around to see Leo Potter. He had walked his horse from the trailer hitched to the back of a ranch truck.

"You and your pals made the front page." He grinned at her.

"Oh that's really nothing. We found one well in town," she lied, "when we were on one of our scavenger hunts."

"I've heard of those hunts." Mr. Potter dropped the reins then loosened the saddle cinch. "They sound like fun." He removed the saddle. "I guess there really isn't much on television in the summer."

Mr. Potter carried Avalanche's saddle to the stallion's stall. The horse turned to follow his trainer. Inside the stall, Leo Potter removed the bridle and hung it on a hook on the wall. Free of the metal in his mouth Avalanche moved his tongue in and out then went over to drink from his trough.

"So what brings you to Mosquito Creek Inn, Ms. Molosky?"

Sonia hesitated. "I'd like to exercise one of the ranch horses. There are two more wells I thought I might check out." She waved her rolled up map.

Mr. Potter looked down at Joker. "You weren't planning to ride out alone?"

"Well…"

Gordon skidded to a stop at the open door of the barn. "You stubborn knuckle-head! I just knew you'd be here!" Gordon threw down his bike and stomped over to where Sonia stood by Mr. Potter.

Mr. Potter laughed out loud. "Okay. I guess we need to exercise two horses." He walked to the tack room and held out two bridles. "Take Copper and Cream Puff, the two at the end." He pointed to the stalls on either side of the open door. Leo Potter brought out two blankets then two saddles.

"Just in case we need to send out a search party, where exactly are you two heading and when do you think you will be back?" The ranch stock manager pushed their bikes to the far side of the barn.

121

"String Falls. That's where the other two wells are located."

Mr. Potter chuckled. "Well I don't see the point. You seem to find people *after* they've been a victim of these open wells."

Sonia and Gordon had ridden almost due west for a mile in a tense silence. Gordon was furious. Scared and furious.

As their horses began a steep climb, Gordon finished what he had started to say back at the barn. "Of all the stupid moves. You took the only map showing the locations of those two wells. What if something had happened to you riding alone?"

"I was going to ask Mr. Potter if he would go riding with me."

"He's the ranch foreman. He'd probably hav'ta work. He's responsible for the livestock. You couldn't count on him to be able to go with you."

"Well, I am not a baby and I have Joker."

Joker stopped at the sound of his name, then he had run on ahead a short distance into the tall grass, as his companions did not seem to need him. Joker continued trotting on with his head down using his nose as his guide.

"*I'm not a baby*" Gordon mimicked Sonia. "I'll remind you for your own good that Zara Grant was older than both of us when she disappeared and she had a useless dog with her as well."

Gordon became quiet again as they turned to take the deer path that lead not just to String Falls but also past the well where Frances Cooper was found. Gordon was unnerved, but logic told him the chances for a repeat of the horror in the coal well, was unlikely.

The shaded woods were cool and peaceful compared with the hot noise of the streets that Mosquito Creek had become with rodeo contestants and so many strangers. One squirrel chased another. They leaped across the path then up two different trees. They scolded the riders then each other.

As the riders approached the well where the remains of Frances Cooper had been discovered, Sonia saw the yellow police tape tied from tree to tree to mark off the area, as an active investigation site. They urged their horses from a trot to a canter passed the taped section of forest.

The forest was deeply shaded as they got closer to the falls. The deer path forked and according to the map they needed to go to the left. The water didn't crash into the stream below. It slid down in a soft, swish as the water dropped straight from the high rocks and then merged smoothly with the swiftly running stream.

"I don't see any sign of where a core sight might have been." Gordon shifted around in his saddle. He and Sonia had ridden eighty yards off the path.

Sonia had lost sight of Joker. "Where is that goofy dog? J-o-k-e-r." She called. She saw grass move and heard bushes rustle before she spotted Joker. He bounded out from beside a wild choke cherry bush, circled her standing horse then headed back the way he came.

"Oh leave him," Gordon suggested. "He's probably chasing a rabbit or skunk, or something."

"Skunk! Yuk! I hadn't thought of that."

They walked their horses a little further off the path then stopped. Gordon looked around again. "Okay. So both wells are up against the same ridge as the falls and on the west side of the falls. They should be here, but I think we'll need to look on foot."

Sonia spotted a twenty-foot mound of dirt the shape of a beehive. The small hill of dirt was over grown with tall grass, wildflowers and wild junipers. "I'll climb up there and see if I can't get a better view of what's around us."

Gordon looked up from the map. "You're wasting your time. You won't be able to spot anything from up there. The growth is too thick."

He watched her struggle to pull herself up the hill. The sides were so steep, that Sonia had to use the branches of low growing bushes to hold onto. On closer observation, Gordon thought the general shape of the hill reminded him of something but he couldn't quite place it. From some angles the hill almost looked cube shaped.

"I made it." Sonia waved from the top. "You look like an ant—wearing blue jeans." She laughed then wandered toward the far side of the hilltop to look.

Gordon had his head down studying the map once again. He didn't see Sonia fall through a thin overgrowth at the center of the mound, he just heard her scream in terror-then silence. Every ounce of his blood seemed to drain to his feet. He felt cold and heavy and couldn't move.

His eyes searched the crest of the mound where he had just seen one of his lifelong friends. "Oh m'God." He slid down from his horse then tried to run. He stumbled in the thick undergrowth. His feet felt weighted to the forest floor.

As he climbed the side of the dirt mound, he too had to use branches to pull himself up. Then he remembered. His grandparents had taken him and his sisters to Alberta, to the Calgary Stampede two summers before. One of the sights they had enjoyed was Heritage Park. The city had recreated pioneer and homestead life just before and just after the turn of the Twentieth Century. At one section of the vast park was a pioneer sod hut. This mound reminded him of that sod hut but this was at least four times the size.

He ran around the top edge of the mound thinking Sonia might have fallen backwards to the ground somewhere on the other side. "Sonia! Sonia!"

Joker sprang from a growth of spruce barking as he raced to the foot of the hill. He ran all around the base trying to find a place he could climb to reach Gordon, but could not.

"Sonia!" Gordon heard coughing, then a faint voice. He called again. "Sonia?"

"I'm…here."

The sound was faint but Gordon followed the sound of Sonia's voice toward the middle of the hill. Sonia had fallen through a flimsy covering of screen door mesh that hid a three foot opening in the earth. He heard Joker whimpering but ignored him.

Gordon peered into the black opening. The skeleton head of Frances Cooper flashed across his memory and he pulled back with a jerk. He took a deep breath then looked again but he still couldn't see anything. "Sonia, are you okay? Have you broken anything?"

Sonia's reply was slow and labored. "I–can't–breath–very–well."

Cold fear washed over Gordon again. "Listen, don't even try to move. I can't see where you are. I left my flash light tied to Copper's saddle. I'll just run and get it."

Gordon stood and turned right into Leo Potter. "That won't be necessary. You won't need a flashlight down there. The circumstances are kind of a shame, but this old trappers' lodge has come in real handy."

He couldn't find his voice. When Gordon looked into Mr. Potter's eyes, there was a savage expression of madness he didn't recognize. Somewhere in the distance he thought he heard Joker barking again.

"Time to join your cousin, and your sweet heart m'boy." Leo hit Gordon on the chin knocking him out. The boy fell backwards into the darkness below.

Joker retreated to the deer path whining and pacing. Leo Potter remounted the trail horse he rode to follow the kids into the forest then took the reins of Copper and Cream Puff, to lead them back to the barn. Urging the horses as fast as they could go on the uneven path, he chased Joker all the way back to the ranch.

Frightened and confused - from the ranch - Joker ran the rest of the way home where he collapsed in the front yard.

CHAPTER SEVENTEEN
Seeing Things

June 28…

The rainstorm moved in swiftly.

Overnight every booth at the fairgrounds was soaked. The soft ground in the events corral was so saturated that the last day of the rodeo had to be cancelled.

All morning the rain pelted the western slopes and foothills of Montana, as the massive weather system spread its havoc from the state of Washington to North Dakota.

No one, in Mosquito Creek, had given any thought to the last day of the rodeo. And even fewer had slept the previous night.

Silas Tate was the one who found Joker. He had returned to town with hogs and turkeys for the rodeo wind-up barbeque when he spotted Joker collapsed on the grass. He pulled his truck over and knocked on the Molosky's front door. Salina and Marc were home with their Aunt Monica playing Monopoly.

Mr. Tate carried Joker to Monica's car. Salina stayed home to try to reach her mother while, Marc went with Monica to take Joker to the veterinarian.

It wasn't until Mrs. McKenna and Eric had returned to Mosquito Creek from their newspaper run through other towns, that anyone noticed

Sonia and Gordon hadn't been seen since they distributed papers around town earlier that afternoon.

As the rainstorm gathered greater strength more booths at the fairgrounds closed early. Eventually, when all of the parents and grandparents finally connected it was just after six-thirty that evening.

Frantic calls to the sheriff's office caused another flashback to the August afternoon when Zara Grant disappeared, seven years before. Swiftly the sheriff organized another massive search party. This time the town had some FBI agents and state police to assist.

Initially the sheriff had absolutely no set clues for a search starting point. So, he assembled several independent teams of searchers. The teams were dispatched to look in multiple directions and places, beginning with the town, the campgrounds and the rodeo grounds - then they fanned out.

****

...June 29...

Grandpa Molosky sipped a shot glass of warm brandy prescribed by Dr. Howes. He hadn't slept. He had been out in the rain all night. He decided to finish the brandy before he went up stairs to talk to his daughter-in-law and her sister.

The doctor returned through the kitchen door. He put his bag down on the seat of one of the chairs. "Mind if I make some coffee?"

Mr. Molosky shook his head.

"Everyone else is resting Gunther. Even Joker is recuperating at the vet's. If I promise to wake you in an hour, will you please lay down at least on the couch?"

Mr. Molosky didn't have the strength to argue with the doctor. He nodded again then headed for the living room.

The doctor watched the brown liquid drip into the pot. He considered that he too might toss a little brandy into his coffee mug. A knock at the back door startled him. It was just past six in the morning.

"Is anybody here?" Sheriff Howard appeared at the rear door. With him were Mayor Peters and Philip. "Aw, doc's making coffee - good call."

Philip skipped across the room straight to the pantry. "Let's have Rainbow Hoops." He announced. Philip counted the number of people in the kitchen.

"Don't forget yourself." His dad reminded him.

Philip grinned. "Oh yeah." He recounted starting with himself. Then he counted out four spoons and four bowls and set the table. Into each bowl Philip shook some of the contents of the box of cereal. He lined up each of the four bowls patting down the cereal to make sure they were all even. Then each person at the table got a bowl.

He helped himself to the milk from the fridge. The milk jug was passed to each person in turn. The doctor poured coffee for everyone but Philip. With a mouthful of pink, blue and green barely pellets, the doctor thanked Philip for fixing breakfast. "I don't believe I have ever had Rainbow Hoops, Philip. This was very thoughtful of you."

Milk dribbled down Philips chin. "You're welcome."

The sheriff wasn't as sure about what he saw floating in his bowl. The milk had turned a very odd color.

The mayor elbowed him. "Dig in Jeff."

No one was surprised that Philip seemed to know where everything was kept in the Molosky kitchen. Philip knew where everything was kept in almost everyone's kitchen all over town.

As he ate, the doctor became a little concerned that with no sleep and Rainbow Hoops for breakfast the day was off to a shaky start. "What brings you here? Any news?"

The sheriff swallowed. "No but Philip gave us a clue."

128

"Really." The doctor addressed Philip. "What's the clue?"

Philip finished drinking the purplish-gray colored milk from the bowl. "Sonia has a treasure map. She got it at Grandfather Sullivan's office."

"How do you know it was a treasure map?"

"It was very old. I told Dad there was no colors on it like the others." Philip hopped off his chair. "Can I watch cartoons?"

The mayor shrugged. The doctor held a finger to his lips. "Be very quiet Philip, Mr. Molosky is asleep on the couch."

"Okay." Philip whispered then tiptoed out through the kitchen door that led into the dining room.

"When the mayor called me this morning we thought that Sonia may have left the map here, or maybe one of the other kids besides Philip saw something."

The doctor cringed. "All the kids are sleeping. I gave their mother and aunt each a mild sedative. This has been a nightmare re-run for their Aunt Monica."

The looked up at the kitchen wall clock. "Just four short hours ago I told everyone to go home and get some sleep 'cause I'd need them to meet back at the fire hall at seven-thirty. I know this is tough but I can't help it doc. You're gonna have to wake each of the Molosky kids so you can ask them if they know anything."

"We don't have a horse returning to the barn on this one. Because of the wells, I called the ranch. The inn manager, Lois Madora didn't see Gordon or Sonia. She was vague about the Knudsen's. She said she'd try to reach them but the wives and the kids left for Minnesota the day before yesterday. She didn't know where Mrs. Knudsen's sons were, but thought they might be in Billings meeting with the ranch accountant."

"None of the other ranch staff saw the kids. The last person I spoke with was the ranch foreman, Leo Potter. He said he didn't see

Gordon or Sonia either." The sheriff stood and stretched. "I'll be at the fire hall. Give me a call if the kids know anything."

****

Bella Perez struggled to wake up. Even with the warm shower water, her eyes didn't want to open. The evening before she had joined the hundreds of police, media and other volunteers, who searched every room in every building, alley corner, park bench and tree branch in Mosquito Creek until two in the morning. And at seven-thirty she had to be ready, again.

The volunteers were asked to regroup to continue the search for eleven-year-old Sonia Molosky, and twelve-year-old Gordon McKenna. She boiled water in the motel kettle to make instant coffee, grabbed a banana then drove to downtown.

When the insurance investigator arrived, the street in front of the fire hall was already jammed with parked cars. Both fire trucks were parked outside. The media were now very visible and seemed to be everywhere, like ants all over cake. The rain wasn't coming down as hard, it had changed to a soft mist but distant visibility was still poor.

The mayor and the sheriff stood on the landing of a set of stairs that lead to the cooking and sleeping area on the second floor inside the fire station. The mayor had the microphone. "Like yesterday, we'll divide up into teams of eight to ten people. Because they know the terrain so well, Paul McKenna will coordinate six teams to the south of the inn, due west of town. Leo Potter has offered to coordinate six teams to the north of the inn."

"Our fire chief, Ken Long will coordinate six teams to search south of the campgrounds on the other side of the highway and east of Mosquito Creek. Frank Whitehead of Montana State Patrol will coordinate six teams to search north of the campgrounds, on the other side of the highway east of Mosquito Creek."

Several reporters scribbled notes, a few held up small tape recorders. The fire hall was filled with residents and visitors. People began to seek out familiar faces of others they teamed with the night

130

before. Each of the coordinators headed for a corner of the hall then divided up their volunteer searchers.

Ms Perez spotted one of the deputies she had searched with the previous night and then followed him to the corner where Leo Potter had gathered his other volunteers.

Mr. Potter saw the deputy and Ms. Perez coming toward his group but kept talking. "I'd like to have everyone head out to the ranch. It will be much easier to meet in the horse barn. From the ranch I can hand out search area locations and maps to each team." Leo stepped down from the chair seat then disappeared out the side door. The people in his group followed.

The sheriff's secretary Mrs. Spear appeared at the side door. She searched the crowd then spotted Paula Lincoln, the FBI agent from the Helena office. When the secretary caught Ms. Lincoln's attention she waved her over to the door. They spoke briefly and Ms. Lincoln disappeared back through the door.

Mrs. Spear then made her way to the front of the fire station and to the steps where the sheriff stood talking to the mayor. She interrupted. "You need to come back to the office - now. Mr. & Mrs. Tate are waiting for you. Their grandson is with them. They say their grandson might know where Gordon and Sonia are."

"What! How long have they been there? So where are the kids?"

"The Tate's showed up just a few minutes ago. But you have to come now! There's a lot more to this than location."

The mayor stayed where he was. "I'll keep everyone moving. Let me know if we need to make changes to the search plan."

Mrs. Spear was a full head taller than the sheriff and closed the distance across the street with less strides than Sheriff Howard. He almost had to run to keep up with her.

The office manager flung open the office door for her boss then all but pushed him through it. Silas Tate with his wife and grandson sat at the round oak meeting table in the sheriff's inner office. As the sheriff entered the room Mr. Tate stood taking off his hat. Mr. Tate's wife and grandson remained seated.

The sheriff sat but Mr. Tate remained standing. " I have a story to tell you. It is a very odd story. Please remember, that Maryanne and I made a decision seven years ago. And - given the same circumstances, I think we would make the same decision again...." Mr. Tate stopped in mid sentence.

Ms. Lincoln came out of the storage room at the back of the office where the copier and the fax machine were kept. She appeared at the door to the sheriff's office with several pieces of paper in her hand.

The sheriff waved to her to join them. "Please Silas continue."

Mr. Tate looked at his wife. Mrs. Tate reached out and touched the sleeve of the young person next to her. As the youth stood up the ball cap was removed. Fine, waist length hair the color of rust fell from beneath the cap. Standing before an astonished sheriff was Zara Grant.

Zara began. "About four hundred yards, south and west of String Falls is an old fur trappers winter quarters made completely from sod." Zara's voice was quiet, but strong. "It's like a small fortress. It's double walled and the only way in or out is through a hole cut in the roof, which is over twenty feet high. The fur trappers used a ladder to climb in and out. Leo Potter and his niece pushed me through that hole and left me there alone and injured, to die."

The sheriff was still reeling from the shock of seeing Zara, alive. "Leo Potter? His niece?"

Ms. Lincoln slid the second page of her fax in front of Sheriff Howard.

The sheriff read the first two paragraphs. "I'm going to lose my mind! Bella Perez? Bella Perez is Leo Potter's niece! She's been in on this from the beginning!"

The sheriff looked at the clock on his wall. "The search party! We gotta get out to the ranch, now. Leo Potter is the one coordinating the search teams in that area."

"I'm coming too." Mr. Tate put on his hat.

The sheriff had collected his wits. "Zara, welcome back. Mrs. Tate, see if you can find Park and Loraine Sullivan, get them down here. Lock the doors to everyone, but Zara's grandparents. Mrs. Spear call the ranch. I'll see if I can get Paul McKenna and some of my deputies on their radios. Paula, will you please stay here?"

Ms. Lincoln nodded. But the sheriff was already heading for the front door with Silas Tate right behind him.

No one noticed that Joey, Hanna, Stephen, Mia and Leif stood just inside the side door to the alley. Mia and Joey had spotted the sheriff and his secretary leaving the fire station. Quickly, they found the others and Mia urged them to follow. The young detectives overheard everything. Then just as quietly as they had come in - they slipped out.

CHAPTER EIGHTTEEN
Four Horsepower

June 29…

Mia had a plan. "We gotta do something. Even if the sheriff can reach Gordon's dad and his other deputies, they'll still lose valuable time."

Joey was anxious to help too. He shivered in the chilled humid air. "Okay, what are you thinking?"

They heard thunder rumble across the foothills. Lightening followed. Then the sound of horses whinnied from the lean-to shelter a block away.

Mia grabbed Joey and Hanna by the hand. Half running, half walking she led them toward the sound of the horses. Stephen and Leif hurried to keep up.

She talked as she went. "When I got to the fire hall with mom and dad, Mr. McKenna was just leaving with two other men. I saw them ride south out of town on horseback." Mia gasped for air as she talked.

"When we snuck into the side door of sheriff's office, I noticed a forestry truck parked at the far end of this street. A man loaded two horses already saddled into a trailer. There may be enough forestry horses that we can b-o-r-r-o-w."

They reached the small holding ring just as Stephen formed his question. "Then what?"

Mia didn't answer. Instead she pointed. "Yes! That's perfect."

The exercise area was only a half circle, closed in on the north by a three-side cement block structure. The shelter was covered by a metal roof open to the corral. Protected from the rain were seven more horses, saddled and tethered and ready.

Mia climbed through the fence, squeezing between the top and the second rail. "Come on."

Joey knew exactly what Mia was thinking. "Brilliant." He was through the fence and following Mia.

Leif and Stephen climbed through next, with Hanna close behind.

The horses sensing excitement whinnied as they watched the young people approach.

Mia untied the reins of the smallest horse. Joey, Leif and Stephen each took the reins of the first horse they came to. Hanna held back.

Still under the shelter of the roof, Mia adjusted the stirrups. "Heading due west, we can be across country and reach String Falls faster than anyone in the search parties."

Joey, Leif and Stephen were in their saddles. The horses lifted their feet stomping - ready to go.

Stephen looked down at Hanna. "Do you need help with the stirrups?"

"I can't go. I don't ride as well as you guys." She looked across the top of the fence toward the foothills. "That's some pretty tough going to String Falls, especially at a gallop. I'll just land on my head."

Mia smiled at her friend. "That's okay Hanna. Open the gate for us and tell the FBI lady we've gone straight across country to String Falls."

"Got it." Hanna ran back to the gate. When she reached it, she swung around to face the riders in a panic. "The gate has a chain and padlock!"

Stephen frowned and urged his mount out of the shelter to the gate. He leaned over and looked. There was a chain looped around the gate post, around the fence post and held fast by a very secure combination lock. "Hanna's right." He looked back at the others and then out over the top of the fence. And his solution came out of nowhere.

"Ye-ha!" Stephen rose up slightly in his saddle and slapped the reins against the horse's hip. Startled the gelding bolted forward toward a section of fence on the opposite side of the ring.

The part appaloosa part thoroughbred reached full stride and cleared the four foot fence with eight inches of daylight to spare. Boy and horse kept moving, gliding west toward the misty foothills at full gallop.

Leif and Joey pressed their heels to the flanks of their horses and together they too bolted out from under the shelter of the lean-to, hooves throwing mud behind them in large clumps. Then up and over, they cleared the fence in unison. With Stephen still in sight, they made a small arch around a stack of covered hay bales then straightened out to follow his lead.

Mia wasn't sure with the muddy ground if her mare could make the jump, but decided she'd give her horse her head, and let the mare decide. With a wave to Hanna, Mia slapped the reins on the flank of her horse too.

Spirited, the smaller horse reared up slightly then shot out across the corral. In one strong, smooth motion, she lifted her rider cleanly over the top rail.

Hanna ran to the fence to watch her friends ride into the mist, crossing open fields at a full gallop - they left safety behind them.

The riders went north then turned west again to cross a narrow bend in Lost Creek. Down the embankment, across the creek then up the other side.

Sensing urgency the powerful horses, skimmed through tall grass with their riders.

The foothills moved toward them.

Swift, long strides ate up ground.

They went up and over fences.

They glided by surprised grazing cattle.

They went down steep gullies.

The sure-footed mounts then scaled lower foothills.

They climbed even higher, to steep switch-back ridges…

Finally with a burst, hooves grabbing earth and lungs heaving the valiant animals reached level terrain at the edge of the mountain forest.

Picking their way between trees, Stephen was still in the lead. His horse seemed to know where to go. Deep into the woods the light was poor but their view was no longer hampered by the foggy mist that hung across the open fields.

Stephen's gelding abruptly hesitated at a grouping of young evergreens. The horse made a quiet snort then stopped, his ears turning. Stephen held up his hand for the others to halt then he dismounted. He heard the sound of metal as he peeked between the evergreen branches. He was amazed to see a familiar deer path on the other side of the stand of trees. He recognized where they had stopped. String Falls was only a few hundred yards to the right.

A movement caught his attention. His heart tumbled in his chest. Just a short sixty feet away he saw Ms. Perez. She slid down the side of a large mound then walked toward two horses tied to trees on the far side of a small meadow bordered by scrub bushes.

Stephen looked for the rider of the second horse. He heard metal again then saw Mr. Potter unwinding a hose attached to an oblong metal canister. Stephen's breathing grew rapid, his vision swam, his stomach churned. His horse turned its head toward Stephen and nudged his arm with his nose.

Jolted, Stephen took in a slow-deep breath to clear his head then tied the reins to a branch. Retracing the way back to where Joey, Mia and his brother waited still mounted on their horses, Stephen kept his voice low.

"Ms. Perez and Mr. Potter are on the other side of those evergreens. There's some kind of hill at the north end of a clearing. Potter's on top of that hill with a canister like the ones they used to fumigate the hotel. We gotta catch'em by surprise. It'll take two of us for Ms. Perez and four of us for Mr. Potter."

Leif raised his eyebrows as he leaned over in his saddle. "Uh, we're short two people."

"I know, but I have an idea."

They listened then Joey too dismounted. He tied his horse to a birch branch and the two boys made their way to the edge of the deer path. Leo Potter's back was to them. Bella Perez was almost to the spot where she and her uncle tied their horses. Her back was to the evergreens that hid the four riders and their horses.

Keeping low, Stephen and Joey crossed the deer path to the base of the hill, unseen. Leif and Mia walked their horses to position. They waited for Stephen and Joey to get in place. Holding on to juniper branches and making a toe-hold in the damp dirt as they went, they climbed up then crouched behind a small pine.

At a gallop, Leif and Mia left the cover of the trees. Startled, Leo Potter looked on for a full half minute still bent over his task as the kids caught up to Bella Perez. In one swift motion they jumped from their saddles and tackled her to the ground.

Leo Potter threw aside the tank of poisonous gas and was about to run to aide his niece when he was jumped from behind and knocked to the ground.

Mia used the reins from her horse to tie Ms. Perez by the hands and Leif used his for her feet. Bella Perez was trapped on the ground, tethered between two horses.

With Bella Perez down, Mia and Leif were on their feet racing with every ounce of energy toward the mound.

Leo Potter had flung Joey off and was on his feet ready to hit Stephen with a rock. Joey got up again and jumped on his back.

Mia reached the top of the mound first and tackled Leo Potter's feet. He went down again.

From his left hiking boot Leif pulled out his lace and Stephen used it to tie Mr. Potter's hands behind his back.

Leif had almost finished taking the laces from his right boot when Stephen tapped his knee, shaking his head. They all looked. Joey had knotted Leo Potter's hiking boots together with his own laces. Joey stood and raised his hands as if he had just roped and tied a calf.

"Help us! Help!" Gordon's voice came from the bottom of the darkness below.

A dog barked. They looked toward the deer path to see Joker running toward the mound. Right behind Joker was Gordon's dad, Paul McKenna with the sheriff, grandpa Molosky - and a young woman with long red hair who looked a great deal like the newspaper photo of Zara Grant!

They could hardly believe what they saw.

The young detectives were astounded even more when they realized two of the other riders in the rescue party, were Douglas and Kevin Knudsen.

CHAPTER NINETEEN
Loose Ends…

THE MOSQUITO CREEK WEEKLY REVIEW   July 5, 1997
Mosquito Creek, Montana   Park Sullivan, Editor

…LOCAL GIRL FOUND AFTER MISSING FOR NEARLY SEVEN YEARS…

While a massive search party was assembling to search for two local children, who went missing June 28 – my granddaughter, Zara Grant presented herself at Sheriff Howard's office at 7:14 A.M. Sunday, June 29th.

Zara Grant went missing under similar circumstances as that of Gordon McKenna and Sonia Molosky – seven years ago, August 16, 1990.

Now 21, Zara turned herself in to local authorities to aide in the search for the two missing children and to also assist in bringing her attackers to justice.

…TWO LOCAL CHILDREN FOUND AFTER FRIGHTENING ORDEAL…

Thanks to the courage of Zara Grant, who came forward after remaining in hiding for almost seven years - Sonia Molosky, 11 and Gordon McKenna, 12 were found only slightly injured.   Zara led rescuers to an abandoned trapper's sod hut located in a remote, wooded area by String Falls. A special thanks also goes to the heroism and quick action of the victims' friends, Stephen Anderlund, Mia Cho, Leif Anderlund and Joey Salas who detained the suspects, Bella Perez and Leo Potter, until authorities could take them in for questioning.

Sonia Molosky suffered a fractured hip and two broken ribs, when she fell 22 feet after being pushed through a hole in the roof, by her assailant.

Gordon McKenna, who had been hit by the same attacker, was unconscious when he was pushed through the single roof opening. Dr. Ralph Howes stated that because Gordon was unconscious when he hit the packed dirt floor of the hut, his injuries were less severe. Young Gordon suffered a mild concussion and a large bruise on the right side of his head.

****

July 7

The day after Sonia was released from the hospital the sheriff made a visit. When the patrol car pulled up to the curb, Sonia was reclining on a patio chaise in the shade of the front porch.

Grandpa Molosky came out through the front screen door carrying two glasses of lemonade. Philip followed right behind him with his own lemonade and a wooden bowl of pretzels.

Philip shot Sonia a mischievous look as he placed the pretzels on the patio table beside her. "The cops! They've come for you! Quick! Run!"

Sonia grabbed a pretzel and tossed it at Philip. "Philip, you're a wretch."

The pretzel bounced off of his forehead. Philip caught it and took a bite. He laughed knowing she couldn't chase him then skipped away across the porch to the top of the steps. "You guys want a lemonade?" He shouted to the street.

Gordon and his grandfather got out of the rear seat of the patrol car. From the front passenger side emerged Zara Grant.

"Not for me, thanks Philip." The sheriff was first up the stairs.

"I'll have a lemonade Philip, please." Mr. Sullivan looked at his grandson and his granddaughter.

"Me too." Gordon nodded. "Thanks."

"Yes please." Zara smiled at the young boy she had last seen when he was three.

Philip vanished into the house at a run.

The sheriff unfolded a lawn chair beside Sonia then took her hand. "How are you doing young lady?"

"I'm fine – really I am. I get to sleep in Grandpa's recliner." She smiled.

"No really," the sheriff persisted. "How are you?"

"Truly, great. Mia and I both talked to Paula Lincoln when I was still in the hospital. I was so scared riding out to the well sight and then Mr. Potter – didn't seem like Mr. Potter any more. Ms. Lincoln said that fear was good. She told us that if we wanted to join the FBI when we finished school, then we needed to be scared. When an agent is scared they're careful."

A second car pulled up at the curb. Agent Lincoln parked behind the sheriff's patrol car. She waved as she closed the driver's door.

Philip reappeared through the front screen door walking very slowly, carrying two full glasses of lemonade. He stopped when he saw agent Lincoln. "Oh great. Now I gotta go get two more. I need ta be one'a those ocapus fish."

Gordon took the glasses from Philip who spun around to make a return trip.

"Hi everyone." Paula Lincoln greeted. Her shoulder length, wavy black hair was tied back with blue velvet cord. Wispy curls framed a round face. Her mocha toned skin was flawless.

The sheriff, Mr. Sullivan and Grandpa Molosky stood as she reached the top of the porch. The sheriff offered the chair beside Sonia.

"Lemonade?" Gordon indicated one of the glasses he held.

"Thank you." She made her way to the other side of a round table then sat in the chair the sheriff left.

When Philip returned the second time he had two empty glasses tucked under each arm and he carried the entire pitcher of lemonade with both hands.

Mr. Sullivan got up to help Philip. "Well done old man. Good thinking."

Philip looked around then asked Grandpa Molosky. "Do we need more pretzels too?"

"No thank you Philip. I think we're fine."

Relieved, Philip squeezed between Gordon and Mr. Sullivan's chairs to take the space beside the sheriff on the porch swing.

"Zara you're looking well. You seem rested." Grandpa Molosky thought the young woman before him was remarkable. He could only speculate as to how her living nightmare had affected her.

"Thank you Mr. Molosky. I am rested. Actually I had seven years to rest." Zara looked at agent Lincoln.

Ms. Lincoln swallowed her lemonade then referred to her notes written on a small pad of paper. "Leo Kohrs Potter and Bella Potter Perez have been formally charged."

Gordon and Sonia were stunned by this news. Their faces showed they were both amazed and puzzled. Gordon blurted out, "Mr. Potter and Ms. Perez were related to each other – and – the Grant family too? Wow!"

Ms. Lincoln smiled then began to explain. "I have some back ground history that even Zara doesn't know, so I'll start first."

"Leo Potter is Bella's uncle. Leo and his father Nelson Potter showed up at the Grant ranch just after Jon Grant returned home from college, in 1970. Nelson Potter was a second cousin to Khors Grant.

By 1950 all of Lester Khor's children had sold their interest in the ranch, left Mosquito Creek to make their lives elsewhere."

"Leo's father was down on his luck and happened to read an article published in *Time Magazine* soon after his mother died. He went through her papers and found some old family photos, so Leo and his father came to the ranch and wanted what they said was their rightful inheritance. Kohrs Grant had no obligation to listen to them but he offered to deed 50 acres located on the southeast corner of the ranch."

"But Leo and his father asked for 1,000 acres and all mineral rights and all of the royalties paid so far, from the 1,000 acres. When Kohrs took back his original offer, Leo and his father found a lawyer willing to sue Khors Grant and Grant Ranch. After two years both Powell County District Court and the Montana State Supreme Court found that neither Leo nor his father had a legitimate claim as all rights to their side of the family holdings had been sold decades before.

"Leo Potter was furious. He was determined to take back what he considered to be - *his* ranch. Leo planned revenge. And his plan was completely ruthless."

Sheriff Howard spoke up. "I already told Park and Zara about this but for everyone else here, we discovered the car accident that killed Zara's parents was engineered by Leo Potter. He waited for winter, so it was fairly easy to make it look like a seasonal accident."

"I was supposed to be with my parents the day they went shopping in Great Falls." Zara added. "But I got the measles and stayed home with my grandfather."

Ms. Lincoln continued. "Leo learned to ride and rope on a ranch in southern Alberta. Using the name of Robert Lake and somewhat disguised with a full beard and moustache Leo Potter made the trip to Mosquito Creek every year for two years to compete in the rodeo. He couldn't take the chance that Khors Grant would recognize him, so he was never in the prize money but he was able to meet Zara."

"I knew him only as Robert Lake." Zara began. "He was very funny and real nice. I was twelve when I first met him and all the cowboys liked Mr. Lake."

"Mr. Lake, I mean Mr. Potter didn't compete in the 1990 rodeo. And when he came to Mosquito Creek he was only here for a day. He told me he had a hip injury and couldn't ride for a while. He also told me he was moving to Montana to get a ranch of his own."

"The next time I saw Mr. Potter was on the deer path to String Falls. He told me he had some land close by and he was out looking for some spring calves that had just been weaned from their mothers. They had wondered off and he asked if I could help him find them. Without thinking, I said yes." Zara began to tremble.

Her grandfather left his chair and stood behind her with his reassuring hands on her shoulders. She took another deep breath and went on. "We rode off the trail and came to a hill that turned out to be the sod hut. I didn't even know it existed, but Mr. Potter had been living there for some time. There was a rope ladder he asked me to climb up to see if I could spot any of the calves in the trees. When I got to the top he was right behind me."

"The look on his face could only be described as wild. His eyes were wide open and I remember they seemed mostly white. He told me I had to go. He said I was in the way of my great aunt and cousins inheriting the ranch. Mr. Potter said my aunt Zigvarta had paid him very well to make me disappear. I saw a rock in his hand and the next memory I have, is waking up to the sound of Mr. Tate's dog barking."

"Mr. Tate's dog is part coyote and has an amazing nose. Anyway, Mr. Tate had been out hunting for rabbits with his grandson. I'd been knocked out for about four days by then. The search party had been all around me but I was unconscious and the rain had messed up the scent for most dogs."

"I had a dislocated shoulder, but no broken bones. I also had amnesia and at first I didn't know who I was. Mr. Tate told me what my name was and wanted to take me home, but I became hysterical then blacked out again."

"Two days later when I woke up, I was in one of the beds in the room the Tate's grandson slept in. My head felt like it was on fire. My shoulder was sore, but back in place."

"Mr. and Mrs. Tate were so sweet. They wanted to get both of my grandfathers, but I didn't want to see anyone. I still didn't know who I was. All I knew was that someone had tried to kill me. I felt safe with the kind old man who found me and his wife."

"I was physically recovering with the Tate's when Mr. Tate came home from town one day to tell me that one of my grandfather's had died of a heart attack. He asked if I wanted to go back to the ranch or did I want to see my other grandfather?"

"All I could feel was the most smothering fear. I knew nothing of any grandfathers or any family. When the Tate's daughter remarried and sent for her son, they took that as an opportunity for me to assume their grandson's place. Since they were fairly reclusive people, no one found their behavior any different than usual."

"As my months with the Tate's past to a year, my memory began to improve, but then Mr. Tate would bring back rumors from town. The three of us talked at length one night. We agreed with Khors Grant gone, I might very well be in even more danger."

"Since we didn't know who meant me harm, it was Mrs. Tate who suggested I just stay with them until I turned twenty-one. At twenty-one they told me I would inherit Grant Ranch and Grant Holdings, and not be under the influence of any guardian. At that time, I still thought I needed to hide from my aunt and my cousins."

Zara was visibly tired. Ms. Sullivan picked up her glass of lemonade and made her take a drink. The cool liquid revived her slightly.

Gordon was impressed. "Zara, Sonia and I know exactly how you felt. We liked Mr. Potter too. We thought he was a friend. I remember that look on his face before he whacked me on the chin."

Zara took another sip of her lemonade. She gave both Sonia and Gordon a weak smile then leaned back into the lawn chair.

Agent Lincoln picked up the story again. "Mr. Potter thought the shock of Zara's disappearance might be enough to kill her grandfather. However when that didn't work, Leo Potter crashed the annual October costume party at the inn. All of the catering staff wore a costume and masks too. Posing as a waiter, he managed to slip powder from finely ground peanuts into the salad served to Kohrs Grant, who was so allergic to peanuts, even a tiny amount caused such a severe reaction that it stopped his breathing."

Sonia and Gordon looked at each other and both blurted out at once to the group. "We knew it!"

Sonia winched as she grabbed her side.

Gordon spoke for her. "We had a meeting of our detective team and we thought Mr. Grant's death was poison. But we were sure it was Mrs. Knudsen and that she had used something from her green house."

Ms. Lincoln smiled then resumed reading from her notes. "With immediate members of the Grant family out of the way, Leo Potter thought all he had to do to complete his scheme was to manipulate some important paperwork. That was where James Clausen came in. There was nobody left at the ranch who might recognize Leo Potter so he presented himself to Mrs. Knudsen as a seasoned livestock manager."

"Then he bribed Mr. Clausen to alter mineral deeds and royalty rights to favor Leo Kohrs Potter. Mia's theory about Frances Cooper was correct. While cleaning Mr. Clausen's office she did see what was going on. When she confronted Clausen, he told Leo Potter."

"That's my first mom." Philip chimed in. "Dad says she was a hero."

"She was very brave Philip. Mr. Clausen was arrested in Oregon yesterday and he spent the first two hours talking his lips numb. He hopes to stay out of prison himself, but that is so very unlikely."

"The finale to Leo Potter's plot was to implicate Zigvarta and her sons in Zara's death. If they went to prison for that crime, they too would be out of the way. To do that, he needed someone on the inside of Mid-Western Insurance. Leo Potter had already paid for his niece's college education. So he had her apply for every job opening that came along at Mid-Western.   When Ms. Perez was hired she focused on getting into the investigation department where she had access to Zara Grant's file."

"The letter that Ms. Perez said caused her to investigate further was made up by her.   Most of the documentation she claimed to have showing flights from Minnesota to Montana were forged or didn't exist."

"The entire scheme was detailed and very deadly.   Four people lost their lives – all for greed.

Philip jumped down from the porch swing.   "I think jail's too good for all of them."   He helped himself to a pretzel for each hand.

Everyone laughed.

Mr. Sullivan nodded as he snatched a pretzel from Philip's hand. "I'm with you Philip."   He waved the pretzel in the air.   "I'm with you."

Mr. Sullivan then took Zara's hand and addressed Gordon and Sonia.   "You two and your other five friends took a huge risk. Huge. But you were relentless and very brave. I like to know the name of your club because the seven of you deserve front page recognition in the next edition of the Review."

Gordon and Sonia looked at each other baffled. Gordon shrugged and blurted, "The Mosquito Creek Detective Club?"

Sonia smiled and nodded. "Oh Mia's gonna love that."

Watch for the return of Mosquito Creek's young detectives in the second episode of this series:

BLACK EAGLE PASS

Made in the USA
Charleston, SC
22 August 2014